Drowned Voice

The Crystal Garden Saga

Drowned Voice

Book 4 of The Crystal Garden Saga

L J Gastineau

Trinity Gateways LLC

DROWNED VOICE,
BOOK 4 OF *THE CRYSTAL GARDEN SAGA*

This is a work of fiction. All characters and events portrayed are fictional, and any resemblance to real people or incidents is purely coincidental.

Cover Art by Blue
Cover Design by Doris Ross

A Trinity Gateways LLC Publication
www.TrinityGateways.net

ISBN: 1941426123
ISBN-13: 978-1-941426-12-8

Dedications

I dedicate this book to my wonderful husband Scott. Thank you for the encouragement and support in following my passion. I appreciate you for all that you do, with all my heart.

Chapter 1

*S*he could not scream.

The earth shook around her as the inky black water surged forward, seeking to consume its victim. The frightened girl clawed at the steep cliff above, but it was no use. Her beloved ocean had been scorned. Soon it would have its revenge.

Panic flooded throughout the terrified blonde, not for her life, but those who were endangered due to her carelessness. If only she'd known what was to come before it was too late!

Salty tears slid down her face as the water crept even closer to her bare feet.

This can't be happening! There has to be a way to change my destiny! Even as she cried she fought to find a way to save herself from the peril that sought to destroy her.

She let out a gasp as the stinging bite of the foam hit her feet before it continued to swallow her whole.

Chapter 2

*M*irielle Riva awoke with a start. She blinked several times trying to bring her blue eyes into focus. Her lips curved into a frown at the unfamiliar room, before her memory filled in the blank.

That's right. She was at the swim team's summer camp. She glanced at the alarm clock then groaned at the time. It was only five minutes before she had to get up. Her blue gaze shifted to her roommate, still blissfully asleep. It didn't seem fair for some reason. Those five minutes of sleep she lost could have made the difference between a good day and a bad one.

Mirielle decided to not disturb the sleeping girl, and instead stayed in bed until the alarm went off.

"Good Morning, Mir!" Isabella Collins chirped in a perky voice. The pretty dark haired girl swept her wavy hair from her eyes, grinning up at the less than enthusiastic blonde.

"Morning."

"This is going to be such a great day. I can feel it in my bones." Mirielle's tall roommate hopped out of bed still in a cheerful mood.

The blonde rolled her eyes. "I'm going to go take a shower. See you in the dining hall."

"Kay!"

Mirielle swept her long mane behind her ears as

she headed out of the room. She didn't mind Isabella, but the girl was too much of a morning person. A part of Mirielle looked forward to the end of the summer camp, while another part dreaded it. There was no telling how long she would be in her newest foster home. That was the problem with being in the system. You never knew where you might live the next day. Some foster parents were the type to keep their charge all the way through adulthood. While others… might turn around and decide that being a guardian to some strange child was too much to handle and as a result would give the child up. At least so far, Mirielle had a little stability. Her foster parents seemed to care for her despite having several kids of their own.

But, she knew not to expect anything. One minute they might talk about adoption, the next, you were packing your bags and waiting to be sent to a 'new' home. The thoughts depressed the blonde teenager. She knew nothing about her birth parents. Only that she had been abandoned on the beach of all places at the young age of two. There was a single fact, which she knew about herself—her first name was indeed Mirielle. That was the little amount of information the little girl could offer. Even now, she pondered why she had been given up.

Stop it, Mir, she scolded herself. She couldn't afford to sink into the depths of despair over her past, at least not now. She had to keep focused to prove that she was good enough for Varsity. Even though she was just an abandoned orphan.

Mirielle was relieved to see the doors to the community bathroom, wasting no time to head straight to the shower, strip then focus on scrubbing herself clean. The spray felt so good that she had a strong urge to sing, yet tried to resist. She didn't want a surprise audience heckling her. Her will-power was short lived as she broke into a cheerful song. Her performance, however, ended on a screech as the hot water went icy cold.

"Wh-" Mirielle began to cry out then froze. She cleared her throat and tried to finish her sentence, but nothing came out. Strange. Her throat wasn't sore, yet she appeared to have caught laryngitis or something. She just hoped that whatever was wrong with her, wouldn't interfere with her swim practice.

Chapter 3

"Open your mouth and say ah," the nurse instructed as she inserted a tongue dispenser in Mirielle's mouth.

What came out of the young swimmer was soundless. Not even a croak could be heard.

The woman frowned. "I said to say ah…"

Mirielle struggled to do as asked, but it was no use. The blonde remained mute. She sighed in frustration. Why was this happening to her? It didn't make any sense. Her throat wasn't sore. In fact, she felt fine, so why did she lose her voice?

After several minutes of examinations and hand writing her replies to various questions, the doctor deduced that she didn't have strep throat, or any other illness that would be deemed contagious. The single diagnosis was she had developed laryngitis. As long as Mirielle didn't strain her voice attempting to talk, it should return in a few days.

Mirielle nodded her thanks, accepting a large pad of paper and a pen as well as a note to her coach explaining her condition before departing from the office. Once outside, she pressed her back to the cheery green wall, annoyed that she was beyond immediate help. Now she was an even bigger freak than before.

At least I can still go to swim practice, she

reminded herself, trying to look on the bright side. In all truth, Mirielle would have rather traded swim practice for having her voice back. Not being able to talk was going to be a major hindrance. She sighed, imagining how her team would react. It wasn't like they all didn't get along, but despite being part of the team, she still felt like an outsider. *Maybe I should just quit the swim team. It's not like I'm anything special.*

"Mir?"

The blonde turned around to discover the captain of her team frowning down at her. Phoebe Keller fluffed out her curling strands of red hair as she studied the shorter girl. "Are you sick with something?"

Mirielle suppressed a groan then mouthed out that she had lost her voice. The older girl only frowned so Mirielle took pen to paper and jotted down what she was trying to say.

"You lost your voice?" Phoebe remarked, staring at the blonde's messy scrawl. "But the doctor said you can still swim? I'm not so sure about that. What if you get the rest of us sick? I don't think I want to chance that!"

Mirielle handed over the note for their coach stating otherwise. Phoebe continued to balk.

"How does she know for sure? If you get us all sick, we might as well kiss State goodbye."

The blonde tried not to glare at her captain. The so called condition, Mirielle was afflicted with didn't make her very happy either. If anything, it left her apprehensive and rather freaked out. She didn't like the idea of brushing off such an odd occurrence as a fluke. Paranoia was getting the better of her the more Phoebe continued to protest. Maybe she should see about visiting a specialist? Of course that would entail finding someone willing to listen to her concerns and take her to one.

"Phoebe," their swim coach, Miss Hall interrupted the girl's tirade as she walked towards the two teammates, her brown eyes narrowed in concern. "Is there a problem here?"

The red head sighed in a way that screamed pure drama has occurred. "Mir is sick."

Mirielle tried to groan, but wasn't granted the luxury to make even a squeak of sound as she handed the woman the note from the nurse.

Miss Hall read it in silence then tucked it in the pocket of her jacket. "It says she's fit enough to swim."

"But-"

"Phoebe, Mirielle has laryngitis. It's not contagious. She more than likely has overused her voice. In either case, if the nurse says she can swim then she will swim."

The team captain made a face, but didn't argue any further. "Fine. If you say so."

"Now, I want both of you to grab some breakfast. You'll need all the energy you can get if we want to beat those Eagles!"

That seemed to make Phoebe stop sulking. "Right! We'll win State this year for sure!"

"That's what I like to hear!" the woman grinned, crisis averted.

Mirielle just smiled as she nodded. She didn't feel the enthusiasm her captain radiated, yet could fake it if it'd keep the red head off her back. She trailed after the girl as she babbled on about her upcoming Senior Year, Homecoming, and Prom.

Chapter 4

"You lost your voice? That really sucks!" Isabella lamented as Miss Hall explained Mirielle's condition.

Cue up violins, the pity party has begun. Mirielle inwardly grimaced as her teammates chimed in with their own versions of sympathy mixed in with a tangle of inquiries, all of which Mirielle had no answers to. She shifted from foot to foot with unease, just wishing they could all shut up and start doing laps. She wanted to concentrate on anything except for her ailment. It didn't help matters that she didn't have her notebook and pen handy. Instead she stood on the pool deck in her swimsuit and swim cap, fumbling with her goggles feeling quite awkward. She doubted things could get any worse.

Miss Hall clapped her hands, vying for the teenagers' attention. "Girls, you can chat later unless you don't want to make it to State this year."

That put an end to the questions the voiceless swimmer seemed to be drowning in. She gave the brunette woman an appreciative smile as they lined up at the edge of the pool, waiting for the whistle blow. Mirielle pulled her goggles over her head, fitting them over her eyes. She knew they were about to start practice any minute now.

With a puff of air, Miss Hall gave them the signal to

begin. Mirielle drew several deep breaths in preparation to dive into the crisp water as she waited for her turn, despite not wishing to take part any longer. The longer she lacked her voice, the less she wanted to enter the pool.

When at last her partner finished her laps, Mirielle bit back her anxiety and dove into the water. As she tried to break through the surface, however, something odd happened—she was unable to find her way back up. It was as though the pool had grown deeper since she entered. Terrified, Mirielle moved her limbs frantically. She didn't want to drown! *What is happening?*

She held her breath as best as she could, ignoring her screaming lungs. The fact that she was stressing out, wasn't benefiting her at all. If she didn't breech the surface soon, she wasn't sure what she was going to do. The day just seemed to get more horrible by the second.

Someone, please help me! Mirielle squeezed her eyes shut, hoping someone would notice her thrashing. To her horror, however, when she opened her eyes, there was no sign of anyone. In fact, she couldn't see anything except water all around her. It was like she had been dumped in some sort of water filled void. *How am I going to get out of here? I don't want to die!*

Just as she began to lose hope, a burst of light from above flooded her vision. Mirielle wasn't sure if she was dead or if someone had come to her rescue. All she knew was that it was her only hope to escape the complete abyss. With that in mind she swam towards it.

Chapter 5

*M*irielle took a gasp of air as she broke through the surface. She almost swallowed the water as she realized that she was indeed no longer at the college swimming pool. In fact, she wasn't sure if she was even in her world anymore. Somehow, she had wound up in what she guessed was an ocean based on the saltiness of the water. It was a good thing she was a strong swimmer. Anyone else might have drowned from the sheer shock of finding themselves elsewhere.

She turned herself in a circle in hopes of finding land. She knew she could not tread water forever. Relief filled her at the sight of what appeared to be a beach a short distance away.

Mirielle swam through the salty ocean water, eager to return to solid ground. She didn't care where she was as long as she wasn't going to drown.

As she waded up to the beach, she froze. Somehow, her school swimsuit had been replaced by a white peasant top with a dark blue corset and a teal and blue print skirt. It was something she had no memory of ever having worn before.

She walked along the beach then paused to squeeze out the excess water from her skirt. This was beyond bizarre! Mirielle wasn't sure if she was dreaming, hallucinating, or had died. Each possibility was disconcerting in its own way.

Now what? She pondered. Mirielle didn't know the first thing concerning what to do in her situation. She wasn't even sure of what label to give it. She was not shipwrecked. Nor was she kidnapped, at least she did not think so. It was all so strange and confusing. Nothing looked familiar. It was all beach, with what looked like a castle in the distance. She squinted at it, but couldn't quite tell what it was. All she knew, was that she had never seen it before either.

Maybe there was a town nearby? Perhaps she could find someone to help her. It was worth a shot, Mirielle decided. Now she just had to walk there. It didn't look too far away.

Feeling a little more optimistic about her predicament, Mirielle began her journey through the thick sand. It wasn't easy walking in drenched clothing, but she wasn't about to complain. After all, she could have died. At least she thought that might have happened. After a few more steps, she could catch a glimpse of what looked like buildings not too far from where she was. Mirielle found herself smiling as she quickened her pace. The opportunity of finding answers seemed too good to be true, yet she couldn't resist feeling a bit of excitement in finding out where she had ended up.

The closer she got, the more she noticed the noises of people going about their days, calling out sales, chattering, or just moving around. Mirielle hoped she could find someone that would be able to help her.

With a deep breath she walked through the open city gates.

Chapter 6

This place is definitely not in California, the teenager thought as she wandered through the quaint little town. It reminded her of something she'd find at a Renaissance Faire, only none of the people had any cameras or cell phones. For some reason that struck Mirielle as strange. Perhaps she was so used to seeing technology everywhere that a single instance without it made her feel like she had set foot on an alien planet. At least from what she overheard, the people spoke English. That would make communicating much easier. Now she just had to find someone who looked like they would be willing to help her.

Mirielle smoothed her still dripping hair away from her face. She wished she could have found something to tie it back with, but perhaps someone would take pity on her being as sopping wet as she was. She walked up to a woman then opened her mouth to say hello, but to her horror, no words came out. In fact, she couldn't seem to make any sounds.

Oh no! Why do I still have my laryngitis? This is bad. Really bad. How am I supposed to find help if I can't speak?

Her heart hammered in her chest as she drew back a step. What was she going to do? She didn't know where she was or how she got there. It was enough to

make her head hurt.

Mirielle spun on her heel and found herself wandering through the little marketplace. Another dreadful thought occurred to her—she didn't even have any money. What if she got hungry? Would someone take pity over a mute girl? Probably not. They didn't even know her after all. Plus, there was no telling how long she would last by herself with no way to communicate. Even if she found pen and paper, she wasn't sure if the people were literate or if things were spelled the same way. They might use the Old English style… or something. Maybe whatever they used in Chaucer? If only she had paid more attention in her English classes! Then again, even possessing that knowledge may not be beneficial either.

In a desperate attempt to avoid a panic attack, Mirielle shut her eyes as she took a deep breath. *It will be okay. You will figure something out just don't lose it. Not here at least.*

Feeling somewhat calmer, she continued walking as she focused on her thoughts in order to keep herself glued together. So what if she couldn't talk. There were worse things. She could still run for instance, which was important if she were attacked. The mere idea of that possibility sent ice down her spine. She was going to be fine. She just had to keep her head. The fear, however, was still not smothered out. If someone tried to hurt her, she wouldn't be able to make a sound. No one would know she was in danger.

Stop it, Mir. You're freaking out over nothing, she chided, in a desperate attempt to snap herself out of her downward spiral. She had to keep her wits or else risk being viewed as mentally disturbed or something. She didn't want to get arrested or worse. There was no telling what might happen in an unknown place.

So, she kept her head up and stayed vigilant. It was

the only way to avoid looking suspicious.

"Hey, you! Girl!"

Mirielle glanced over her should then froze at the sight of a dark haired young man with deep green eyes staring at her.

He shoved at his tangle of hair flitting about his face, studying her closely. He scowled at having received no response, but seemed to shrug it off. "Did you fall overboard or something?"

Or something, Mirielle grumbled in her head as the man chuckled at her. She wished she could give some sort of verbal reply. Instead she lifted her shoulders with her eyes narrowed in annoyance.

"Talkative, aren't we," he commented in a sarcastic tone. "Look, I was just wondering why you were soaked to the bone, but if you want to be rude then that's fine by me."

Mirielle mouthed that she had lost her voice, but he didn't appear to be able to read lips. She pressed a hand to her forehead in frustration. This was not going well at all. She sighed then motioned to her throat as she mouthed that she couldn't talk.

"So, you're mute, huh. That's a shame. I was hoping you'd prove to be more interesting," he said, earning a heated glare. "Don't look at me like that. I just wanted to know why you look like a drowned rat- not that you're rodent like!"

Gee thanks. Listening to you is a big waste of my time. I should find someplace else to go. The question is, where? Forget it. Anywhere is better than here, she thought, growing more irritated the longer she listened to the stranger. Refusing to allow him another minute of her time, she spun on her heel and stomped away.

Chapter 7

The nerve of that guy! Who does he think he is? So what if I'm dripping wet from the stupid ocean. Is that even any of his business? Is he the fashion police or something? Was I breaking some sort of law? Mirielle clenched her jaw tighter the more she reflected on her prior encounter with the strange young man. She knew how to deal with guys, but never had the displeasure of interacting with one so... annoying! If she had a voice, she would have given him a piece of her mind, but no, she wasn't granted such a luxury. This had to be the worst day of her life.

She came to a halt once she put enough distance between them. The blonde was in enough of a predicament dealing with her muteness as it was. She didn't need even more stress on top of what she was already going through. Unfortunately, Mirielle had no clue on how to solve her problems. She had no idea where she was or how to communicate that she needed help. She had no money so even buying something to write with was out of the question. Everything seemed to be growing more problematic by the second. *I need a miracle.*

"Hello! Are you who I think you are?" A small voice seemed to whisper to her.

Great, now I'm hearing voices. Can this get any

better?

"Violet, what are you doing?" A different, slightly deeper voice inquired.

"Quiet, Zandr. I believe I know her."

Just as Mirielle was about to run, two fairies appeared in front of her, one female, wearing pink and the other male with dark hair dressed in gray. The female one smiled as her amber eyes shone with recognition.

"I do know you!"

Mirielle frowned. She had no clue fairies even existed until that moment. How could one know who she was? *Maybe this is all a bad dream after all…*

Violet fluttered in front of the confused blonde then tilted her head as she studied the girl. Her strawberry blonde curls bounced with the movement. "I guess you don't remember me. It's all right. I was where you are before."

Wait, what? What is she talking about? The swimmer groaned, wishing she could wake up or at least go back to her world. She didn't care so much about getting her voice back as long as she could find answers as to what was going on.

"My name is Violet," the fairy began. "Anyway, I can tell that you are a bit bothered by what is going on, which is perfectly understandable."

That's the understatement of the century, Mirielle thought in agitation.

"Are you going to mention, what I think you are?" Her companion inquired, earning a glare.

"Yes, it is only fair." She gave Mirielle a smile as she gestured to the raven haired fairy "That is Zandr by the way. Anyway, you need to seek out the Crystal Garden. I know it sounds odd, but it will explain a lot about who you are and why you are here."

Mirielle's lips curved into a frown. That was a new

one.

Violet blinked in surprise. "Judging by the look on your face, you either are just really quiet or can't talk."

The blonde nodded as she put two fingers up indicating the second possibility was correct.

"I'm sorry to hear that. I'll tell you the same thing the others have—if you make it to the Crystal Garden, repay the favor by looking to help a girl named Lunette. She may not sound familiar to you now, but she will eventually. Also, if you come across two girls, one with dark hair and the other brown who go by the names Bianca or Cybele, they are also friends and may be able to offer their aid as well."

Mirielle nodded again. It was the best lead she had so far. The only problem was that she had no idea how to go about her search. Her lack of speech was making a bigger hindrance by the second.

"I wish I could be of more help…" Violet trailed off as though something caught her eye. "Perhaps taking that boat wouldn't be a bad idea. It'd be quicker than going on foot."

"Violet-"

"It's the best suggestion I have," she finished in a hurry, giving Zandr a look that warned him not to interfere. "It was nice seeing you, but it looks like that ship is about to leave and it would be best for you to be on it. Good luck!"

Mirielle frowned as the fairy zoomed off, dragging her companion behind her. *That was just odd. But I guess taking a boat is my only option other than wandering around blind. Maybe I can find someone who can help me.*

With that thought in mind, Mirielle headed towards the docks.

Chapter 8

It didn't take Mirielle too long of a walk to get there. Unfortunately, Violet was correct about the ship she had gestured to. It was almost ready to leave. Mirielle wasn't fond of the idea of sneaking aboard, but without money, it was the only choice she had. At least if they caught her and threw her overboard, she was strong enough a swimmer that she should survive just fine. Unless she came across a shark, or they had other ideas for punishment. Great.

She didn't want to be assaulted or worse, but it was her only option, or so it seemed. Then again, how did she even know she could trust the fairy? Weren't fairies known as pranksters in some parts of the world? What if this was all one big set up to get her hurt in order to entertain the mischievous trickster? Mirielle's stomach turned at the thought. Maybe there was another way to get where she needed to.

"Hey! What are you doing?"

Mirielle spun around then almost gave a shout of frustration at the sight of the same man that had irritated her earlier in the small town.

His dark hair blew away from his scruffy face in the breeze. He tucked a hand in his jacket pocket and smirked. "Just couldn't keep away from me, could you, sweetheart? Name's Dmitri by the way. Guessing you're still giving me the silent treatment."

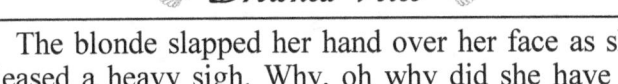

The blonde slapped her hand over her face as she released a heavy sigh. Why, oh why did she have to run into him again?

"I see you're checking out my girl. She's a real beaut' my *Mermaid Princess* is..."

Mirielle's eyebrows winging up as she took notice of the carved mermaid christening the bow. The resemblance to her own features was uncanny.

"So you noticed it too. Funny how the world works," Dmitri chuckled, placing an arm around the blonde's shoulders. Mirielle shoved it off earning a snort. "Even more amusing, is I was told to dock here today, but not given a reason why, yet, here you are, looking just like the girl on my ship. So tell me, who are you really?"

His answer was complete silence until, after much debate, Mirielle moved her hand like she was writing.

This time Dmitri understood. "You need parchment and a quill. Step into my shop. I believe I have just the thing."

Mirielle hesitated then followed him on board. So far, other than being a bit of a flirt, the guy seemed harmless, even kind of charming to a degree. She just hoped she wasn't going to regret her decision.

Chapter 9

The *Mermaid Princess,* was a far more intriguing ship than it appeared from the docks. Even though it wasn't a large ship, it was still well manned with a lot of activities on the main deck. She could see the white flags hanging off the masts bellowing in the breeze.

Dmitri grinned as he noticed Mirielle's look of awe. "Nice to see some appreciation for my girl."

Unable to give a reply, Mirielle instead gave the man a small smile. Then she mimicked writing, in hopes he didn't just want to bring her on board to show off.

"Haven't forgotten about you either, sweetheart. Just wanted to give a bit of a tour is all," he gave her a wink which made her cheeks feel warmer than usual.

The blonde shrugged off the strange sensation as she trailed after him to the Captain's Quarters.

The room was quite neat with a large table where several maps lay strewn about as well as a few bottles, among other trinkets. Dmitri picked up a leather bound book, tore a few pages out then handed it and a quill to her. "These should do the trick I would think. So can you finally solve a mystery for me by giving your name?"

Mirielle rolled her eyes, but did as he requested, handing over the book.

"Mirielle. Pretty. Kind of rolls off the tongue. I think I kind of like Mir too. I'll probably call you by both... although, sweetheart suits you as well." He smirked as he added the last part. "So what's your interest in my ship and please don't tell me you were planning on stealing it, because that would just break my heart."

She raised her eyebrows at him, but wrote her response explaining what Violet had told her including the Crystal Garden.

"A fairy, huh. Can't say I've heard that one before. The Crystal Garden on the other hand... isn't that a myth?"

Mirielle shrugged her shoulders.

"And while we're on the topic, why can't you talk or have you always been mute?"

She sighed then scribbled down that she had lost her voice but didn't know why or how to get it back.

"That's unfortunate. I bet you must have the voice of an angel."

Mirielle blushed. She never thought much about what she sounded like, but angel seemed far from the truth. She wrote one more thing. *Are you going to help me?*

Dmitri nodded. "I told you, I was sent here and by the looks of things, I think it may have been to find you... as strange as that might sound."

Mirielle wrote 'thank you', as she smiled in appreciation.

The sailor gave her an awkward smile back as he scratched the back of his head, hiding a slight flush. "Don't mention it."

Just then a small orange blur caught Mirielle's eye. She spun around and was stunned to see an orange tabby scamper into the room then leap up on the table where he continued his ascent to Dmitri's shoulder.

The ship's captain laughed as the kitten licked at his scruffy cheeks.

"Easy, there, Pounce. I wasn't gone that long, buddy." Dmitri caught Mirielle's amused look then grinned. "Pouncer has been with me for a few months. He's a great mouser who I happened to find outside of a pub one evening. The little furball and I hit it off so, he's been with me since."

Mirielle couldn't help, but find Dmitri's interactions with the cat rather endearing. It was something she least anticipated, yet was delighted to witness. Pouncer's happy purring seemed to warm her heart as Dmitri stroked the feline's silky fur. It was clear that the two were quite fond of each other. Just the sight made Mirielle long for a pet of her own— something she was never granted.

"Ow! Watch the claws," Dmitri warned Pouncer who gave a meow in response. "He gets a bit over enthusiastic at times."

After a moment's hesitation, Mirielle reached a hand towards the feline. Pouncer sniffed at it before rubbing his face against it as he purred with more vigor. She smiled at the affectionate noise the little kitten made.

"Looks like he likes you too," the captain commented, with a knowing look. "Not surprised. He is a good judge of character after all. Tell you what, you hold onto him and I'll get us on our way."

Before the blonde could think of a response to write down, Dmitri picked up Pouncer and handed him off to her.

"Don't worry. He's not going to tear into you as we set sail. He actually enjoys it, strange cat," he added with a brief ruffle of fur before dashing towards the door. "You can come up with me or stay down here. It's your choice. Pounce doesn't care either way."

Mirielle chewed on her bottom lip in thought then decided, why not? It was her first time on a ship. Might as well make the most of it. She gave Dmitri a nod then followed him on deck. She was beginning to looking forward to what her adventure had in store for her.

Chapter 10

The sheer energy it took to set sail was enough to make Mirielle's head spin. Dmitri's crew moved with a swift, efficient force. The *Mermaid Princess* may not be a large ship, but it still took a bit of man power to get her moving.

Pouncer purred in her arms as she watched the crew in action. She had to admit, Dmitri was quite capable of taking command, something she hadn't expected the first time they met. Now however… she still wasn't sure of what to make of him or if she should trust him, but he was her only chance in getting to the Crystal Garden.

Plus he's not such a jerk after all. Mirielle decided as she petted the kitten.

It wasn't long before they were heading towards the open seas. Mirielle couldn't help, taking in the view as the breeze blew the salty spray in her face. She found it rather invigorating. It had been a long time since she had last gone to the beach. A frown curved on her lips as she tried to remember when. It must not have been too long, since she could still recall moments of running on the sand and swimming in the crisp clear water. Perplexing enough, she couldn't place her finger on a particular date. It was disconcerting the more she thought about it.

"Enjoying yourself?" Dmitri inquired as he joined

her.

Wishing she had the ability to talk, and not wanting to risk tossing pages or splatting herself with ink, Mirielle gave him a smile as she nodded.

"I bet you aren't too happy, I mean with not being able to talk. I can't imagine how rough it'd be…"

Mirielle lifted a shoulder, not wanting to admit that he was right. She never realized how much she took talking for granted. It was natural, just like hearing and smelling, but to go without it after being accustomed to it after so long was quite devastating if she were to be honest with herself. Still, Mirielle tried to cope the best she could and so far, she was handling it.

"Sorry, I shouldn't have even brought it up. It's none of my business." He rubbed at his chin as though feeling uneasy. "I'm not trying to upset you. I was just curious. I'll bet you'll be glad when we reach port so you can be rid of me."

She frowned, not expecting him to say such a thing. She couldn't blame his need to ask questions. If the tables were turned, she might have voiced the same thing. She also wasn't sure if she liked the idea of traveling alone. Even though she didn't know Dmitri well, he didn't seem threatening. Plus if he knew anything about the Crystal Garden, he might be able to help her on the quest.

Just as Mirielle was able to head into the cabin for her parchment, the ship began to rock violently. She spun around then gasped at the sight of the pitch black sky looming overhead as the waves grew choppier.

"Where did this storm come from?" Dmitri yelled, in frustration as he raced for the helm.

Lightning flashed, striking the main mast, sending it crashing down into the poop deck. The crew scattered, some struggling to keep the ship afloat while others attempted to extinguish the flames. All Mirielle could do was watch in horror as she hugged a terrified Pouncer to her chest.

Another bolt struck the forecastle deck, setting yet another fire to the already battered ship. The impact of it and a gigantic wave was enough to send the *Mermaid Princess* to her doom. Mirielle had mere seconds to take a gasp before a pain flooded her skull as she fell into inky darkness.

Chapter 11

The first thing Mirielle noticed was a bright light. The next thing was that she was no longer on a boat. Or in the ocean for that matter. She frowned at the fact that she wasn't even damp. *What... happened? Am I dead?*

"You're in your mind," a blonde girl wearing a lavender dress explained as she stepped towards to confused swimmer. "And no, you're not dead."

Mirielle opened her mouth to speak, but no words would come out. *Why can't I still talk? This doesn't make any sense!*

"It is the spell you're under. It took away your voice. You do know who you are really, don't you?"

Mirielle's brows knit together as she shook her head. She couldn't seem to shake the unease at finding herself alone with another girl in what appeared to be some sort of void. Everywhere she looked, it was all white with nothing else around them.

"Think. You love the water and lost your voice..."

The confused swimmer shrugged.

"You are the Little Mermaid."

Mirielle's blue eyes widened in complete bewilderment. *That's impossible. I'm not a mermaid! I have legs. It's just-*

Her mind drifted to the mermaid on Dmitri's ship. There was just something about it that made her begin to doubt her words.

The stranger toyed with her long curls as she gave her companion a mysterious smile. "Does it seem that farfetched? Especially having a quest to find the Crystal Garden?"

Mirielle's jaw almost dropped. How did this person know and how were they even communicating if it was all in her head?

"Don't seem so alarmed. I'm just like you, except I'm stuck in a sort of limbo until my time comes. My name is Lunette by the way. There is a chance when we meet outside of dreams that I won't remember this, but you on the other hand will," she paused a moment then added. "Oh, and Dmitri… Your gut instincts are correct—you can trust him. Just be cautious about those around you."

If Mirielle still had the ability to talk, she had a feeling that she would be at a loss for words. So this was Lunette—the girl Violet spoke of? Mirielle had to admit, she did seem to be following her gut with setting foot on Dmitri's ship. She was never one for taking risks, especially when it came to strangers. The fact that she went with him and did not consider every single consequence beforehand was absurd.

Lunette smiled. "Find your Crystal Rose and you'll have your answers. In the meantime, keep your faith. You're doing well so far. We will meet again."

Before Mirielle could react, the room dissolved into darkness.

Chapter 12

*M*irielle tried to take a large gulp of air and regretted it as she sputtered, choking on the sea water that still lingered in her lungs. Strong hands helped her turn over as she regurgitated the water she had inhaled.

"Slow, deep breaths. Take it easy, Mir. You're okay," a deep voice soothed.

It was difficult, but she did as she was told. After a moment, she opened her eyes to find a soaked Dmitri leaning over her with a drenched, unhappy looking Pouncer clinging to his shoulder. The orange tabby looked miserable.

Mirielle tried to push herself up, only to have Dmitri hold her back.

"I said to take it easy. You just about drowned for crying out loud!" He took a breath of his own and apologized as he lowered his head. "I should not have yelled, I… wasn't sure if you were going to make it. Just before my ship began to sink you got hit in the head by a chunk of the foremast. It knocked you out and I almost didn't reach you in time. Sorry."

She stared at him, taken aback by the emotion in his voice. It was something she wasn't sure how to respond to, so she mouthed the words, 'Thank you.'

Dmitri nodded, his wet hair splashing droplets of water with the movement.

The cat on his shoulder leaped down with a hiss then began grooming himself, glaring every once in a while at the captain.

"Hey, it's not my fault the ship went down," Dmitri grumbled then took a handful a sand and threw it in a fit of rage. "That shouldn't have happened! She was mine!"

Mirielle sat up. She was still catching her breath, but felt more concern over her companion. He seemed to be taking the loss of his vessel rather hard. She wished she knew what to do for him, but words were beyond her power. So instead she reached out and touched his arm.

He turned then looked at her. His obvious surprise over the gesture was written all over his face, yet he didn't pull away. Instead he sighed—the anger melting away. "She- my ship, was all that was mine. I took good care of her. Better than my brother would. She was my life and now… she's gone."

Mirielle glanced around, expecting to see the other crew members, but she, the captain, and the kitten were the only ones on the sandy beach. Did all the men drown? Sorrow filled her heart at the mere thought.

As if able to read her thoughts, Dmitri shrugged. "Everyone's gone. I'm not sure if they died or were swept away elsewhere. At least I was able to save you."

He must wish deep down he never met me. Maybe if he hadn't taken me aboard, his ship wouldn't have sunk. Mirielle knew her thoughts were ludicrous. After all, how could she be liable for a freak storm? Then again, if what Lunette had told her was true, then perhaps she was to blame.

Dmitri climbed to his feet then offered Mirielle his hands to help her up. Once she accepted he gave her a small smile. "The plus side is, we aren't alone. I'm not sure where we ended up, but I know that the adventure wouldn't be half the fun without a pretty girl by my side."

The blonde felt herself blush. She wasn't used to compliments, and wasn't sure if he was being serious or just playing with her to distract himself from the devastation they had just experienced. Instead she gave him a shy smile.

The captain knelt in front of Pouncer and offered his arm. "You still mad, or do you want to come with too? I doubt you'll find any mice here."

The kitten glanced up at him, then with a meow, jumped up onto Dmitri's arm. It wasn't long before he clamored up to the captain's shoulder, where he sat, purring.

"That's what I thought," Dmitri chuckled at the feline who rubbed against his face despite the wetness. He turned to Mirielle and smiled. "Shall we?"

She nodded, as she joined him.

Together they headed up the beach, hoping to find something or someone that could tell them where they had washed up. The sooner they got those answers, the better off they would be.

Chapter 13

They had walked for close to a mile before Mirielle's stomach began to growl. Dmitri glanced at her in amusement, and she felt a flush spread over her face. Despite the embarrassment, she couldn't blame her body for reacting in such a way. After all, she had no clue how much time had passed since her last meal.

"It seems someone's hungry, or you're a werewolf and didn't tell me," he teased.

Mirielle wished she was able to talk, instead she just narrowed her eyes at him.

"Come now, that was funny!"

She just sighed, then pondered if they might come across any berries or other edible foods that came from nature. *Of course, how would I know what is safe or poisonous? I doubt Dmitri has a merit badge in botany.*

"If my ship hadn't gone down, I could have fed you something," Dmitri commented, his green eyes hard with the memory. "So instead, we'll have to see if I remember my schooling. Lucky for you, my worse subject was English."

Pouncer's ears perked up then he darted off towards a bush. He looked back at the pair, mewing with joy.

"Or we can trust the cat."

Dmitri and Mirielle approached the feline's bush, examining the dark colored fruit. The captain let out a chuckle. "He found blackberries. Smart cat. Thank you."

The reply was a simple meow before Pouncer batted one off the vine before chowing down.

Mirielle knelt down and claimed a berry of her own. She would have preferred washing it, but there was no telling how long it would take them to find fresh water. Plus she was quite hungry. She smiled at the sweetness, then took another.

The trio ate in silence, clearing out the fruit from several bushes until they had their fill. Dmitri wiped his mouth with the back of his hand. "Not exactly the most satisfying meal, but it will do."

And we'll be hungry again in an hour, his companion thought, adding onto his comment. Still, it was better than nothing, Mirielle decided.

Pouncer licked at his paws in a desperate attempt to remove the berry stains from white fur. Dmitri laughed, at the perturbed feline. "You should have been more careful, Purple Toes."

The orange tabby let out a pitiful meow as though begging Dmitri to fix the problem.

"We'll find you some soap, but in the meantime you'll just have to deal with it."

Pouncer dug his front paws in the dirt then let out a grumble at having dirtied himself. His furry face contorted into an agitated expression as he began cleaning himself again.

Dmitri shook his head. "Funny little cat."

Mirielle bit her lip, amused by their antics. It was clear that Pouncer would be lost without Dmitri and the captain might feel the same. They needed each other. Mirielle wasn't sure where she might fit in if at all. She just hoped that she wasn't a burden.

"We should get a move on before your stomach decides to make itself known again," Dmitri said to the blonde, who raised her eyebrow at him. "Okay, fine. Mine too. And Pounce's."

"Meow." The kitten circled Dmitri's legs, pleased to have not been left out.

"Shall we?"

Mirielle nodded, joining him on yet another trek through the woods. She hoped they'd find civilization soon. She wasn't used to hiking.

Chapter 14

$\mathcal{M}$irielle sighed, growing tired of their constant walking. It didn't help that Dmitri was quiet for much of the journey. She wondered at what he had said earlier about his ship and his brother. She wanted to know more, yet was unable to ask. A part of her wished he would start talking again since she was growing tired of the quiet, bored.

She tried to focus her attention on the scenery, but she was never one for taking going on nature trails. She liked nature, but preferred the water over anything else. Her lips curved into a frown as a thought struck her. *Maybe I am the Little Mermaid, after all.*

It was odd to even consider it. Then again, how did she go from the swimming pool to the ocean? It didn't make much sense. The more she thought of it, there was very little that made much sense.

"I'd ask you, what you were thinking about, but I don't have anything you could write with," Dmitri murmured, observing how she was gazing off into the distance.

Mirielle shrugged. She could tell that Dmitri wanted to know more about her, however, her lack of voice made it quite difficult.

He put a hand on her shoulder. "Hey, we'll find a way to get your voice back. Don't worry."

She gave him a tiny smile as she nodded. At least

he understood and even wanted to help her. It was more than what she was used to. At least she didn't feel unwanted. It was nice not being alone. She wasn't sure how she would handle being shipwrecked by herself. Then again, she might not have made it to shore. She might have drowned if Dmitri hadn't saved her. Did that mean he had to give her CPR? Her face reddened at the thought of his lips pressed against hers. *Stop acting like a silly school girl. He only did it so you wouldn't die! There was no make out session involved.*

"So…" Dmitri removed his hand, then rubbed at his face. It was something that Mirielle was noticing a lot more of the longer they were together. "I know you can't talk, but you can nod and shake your head. That's something. I bet you never expected we'd get shipwrecked."

Mirielle shook her head as she smiled. He did have a point. She may not be able to use her voice, however, her neck muscles worked just fine.

He lifted his head to the sky as though trying to come up with another question. "Ever been on a boat before?"

She was about to shake her head then froze. A part of her wanted to say yes, but she didn't have the memories to go with it. Unsure of what answer to give, she shrugged.

"You don't know?" He raised an eyebrow at that then lifted a shoulder. "I guess you mean you don't remember. That's feasible."

Mirielle bopped her head, glad he had found some logic to her confused reply. She wasn't sure how she would have done trying to translate if Dmitri was the one to have lost his voice instead. She imagined she may not have caught on as expedient as he did though. It was a wonder she was able to figure out ways to

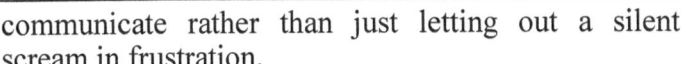

communicate rather than just letting out a silent scream in frustration.

Her thoughts shattered when Dmitri grabbed her hand. It was unexpected and set her heart thundering in her chest.

"Did you hear that?"

Before either of them could react, five men appeared from behind the shadows of some large trees. Each brandished either a cutlass or other sharp pointy weapon and a menacing sneer.

"Well, looky what we got here…" one of them remarked with an evil glint in his eyes. "Looks like we might have found ourselves a little entertainment, boys."

Chapter 15

*D*read bubbled in Mirielle's stomach at the sight of the greasy looking strangers who smelled in dire need of a good scrub down. The odor of rancid fish almost made her vomit up her earlier meal. She inched closer to Dmitri as Pouncer hunched over, ears flattened in fear. If she could judge the situation based on the kitten's reaction alone, Mirielle would say that they were in deep trouble.

"Nice day for a walk," Dmitri chuckled, in an effort to hide his uneasiness. He angled himself to keep his body between the men and Mirielle. "But I think we would fare better elsewhere, so if you would excuse us…"

"You ain't going anywhere," the stocky bearded man drawled, pointing his cutlass at Dmitri. "Not until we decide that we're done with you."

Dmitri narrowed his gaze. "Look, we don't want any trouble. At least let the girl go. You can do what you want with me instead."

Pouncer took that opportunity to hop onto Mirielle's shoulder then continued to cower.

"We'd rather take the girl and leave you instead. She's a lot prettier."

Ice ran down Mirielle's spine as the men leered at her. The urge to run made her skin feel as though it were on fire. She had to get them out of there before it was too late. The question was how?

"She's innocent!" Dmitri protested, in a desperate attempt to protect the blonde.

"We just want to hear her scream," the tall dirty blonde man stated then licked his lips.

Fat chance since I lost my voice, Mirielle thought, not appreciating the threat in the least. If only she knew somewhere they could go for help. It was unfortunate that neither she nor Dmitri seemed to know where they were. That made things quite complicated. They might be on a deserted island with no possible means of escape. She hoped they would find a way to escape from the dangerous circumstances they had found themselves wrapped up in.

Dmitri's body went from ridged to almost calm as he said, "Wrong answer."

Before the strangers were able to react, Dmitri brandished a cutlass, striking the man nearest to Mirielle just before a grubby finger could touch the girl's skin. The would-be-attacker dropped his rapier as he clutched at his handless wrist screaming in agony.

The remaining men charged at Dmitri who did his best to defend.

"Run, Mir! Get out of here!" He tossed over his shoulder to the frightened blonde girl.

Mirielle wanted to escape more than anything, but her feet refused to move. It was an unfair fight for Dmitri. The likelihood of him coming out on top was slim. She couldn't just leave him to sacrifice himself for her. Mirielle's deep blue gaze fell upon the now sobbing man's abandoned weapon. She had seen sword fights before so she knew that a rapier was more of a thrusting weapon, best suited for stabbing, not cutting. She didn't know if she'd be of any help, but she had to try.

Pouncer hopped down and scampered up a tree. His instincts that Mirielle was about to put herself in danger were right on.

With determination flowing through her veins, she picked up the weapon and struck out at the dirty blonde man.

He growled a curse before slashing at her with his sword. Mirielle evaded, dodging to the left then jabbed at him, sticking his right shoulder. The man howled in pain, and rather than attack with his weapon, backhanded her hard enough to see spots.

"That is not how you treat a lady!" Dmitri was on him, having dispatched the other three men. With a swift movement, he sent his fist into Mirielle's attacker's face, breaking his nose with a sickening crunch. The man's eyes crossed before he collapsed.

Mirielle stared in shock for a moment then glanced up at Dmitri. He had a few scratches on his face, but he didn't look worse for wear.

"Are you all right," he inquired, looking her over. "They didn't harm you?"

She shook her head.

"Then let's get out of here. I'm pretty certain they were pirates which means there may be more of them. So you better hang on to that," he added, gesturing to the rapier. He walked to the unconscious former owner then removed the belt and scabbard. Dmitri held it out to Mirielle who looked stunned. "He has no need for it anymore."

She gave a nod, accepting the offering. She wrapped the belt around her waist, securing it with the buckle. These were bad people, Mirielle had to remind herself. *Those men don't deserve pity. They would have hurt and/or killed you and Dmitri. They did this to themselves.*

With that thought in mind, she sheathed the sword.

Together they checked through the pockets of the men, retrieving a small amount of money, some food, and several weapons including a whip. Mirielle stared at the weapon as though there was something about it that struck her.

"Do you want it?" Her companion inquired, snapping her out of her daze. "I was going to get rid of the ones we don't plan on taking with us just in case."

To her surprise, she nodded yes.

As he held it out to her, he gave her a hair comb decorated with small shells and starfish. His face colored as he added. "Found this. Thought it'd suit you."

Mirielle's cheeks warmed as she took it in her hands. She couldn't recall owning something so beautiful before. Unable to help herself, she put it in her hair.

Dmitri's blush deepened, but instead of saying anything he walked to the tree where the kitten was still hiding. "Come on, down, Pounce. They're not going to hurt you."

Pouncer gave a tiny meow as if disagreeing.

"We're going to leave without you... Come on, buddy. I'm not going to let anyone harm you. I promise."

The feline hesitated then jumped down, landing on Dmitri's shoulder who hissed in pain.

"Claws! We've been through this before!"

Pouncer ignored the protest. Instead he wiggled under the back of Dmitri's coat collar.

"Just don't turn me into a pincushion," he sighed, then held out a hand to Mirielle. "Ready?"

Mirielle was so distracted by the captain and his cat's antics that when Dmitri offered his hand, she froze. Her mind chided that he did it to make sure he didn't lose her which seemed quite logical. It didn't, however, calm her nerves. Regardless, she accepted. Dmitri probably felt responsible for her. There was no possible way that there was more to it than that.

With her mind whirling on the potential reasons he wanted to hold her hand, they started off again.

Chapter 16

She needed to get her mind off him or else she was going to go insane. Mirielle had to admit, the more she was around Dmitri, the more she enjoyed his company. It was different being around someone who seemed to care and wanted to make sure she was comfortable. Every once in a while he'd ask how she was holding up. The thought made her smile. His concern for her appeared to be genuine.

Don't start, Mirielle. This is not the time to go gaga over a guy that you don't even know. You are in some strange place and can't talk. He is only here to help. There is nothing more to it, so grow up and stop going all gooey over him.

Mirielle drew in a deep breath after the harsh berating of herself. She had to be practical after all. This wasn't a vacation—not that she had ever been on one before. That was beside the point. She just couldn't let her teenage hormones distract her. Even now, although she was armed, she was still a liability because she had no voice.

Now that she thought of it, that explained why Dmitri wanted to hold her hand—he didn't want to risk them getting separated. Plus if she got into trouble, he'd never know because she can't make a sound. *See, nothing more to it.*

The realization, however, made her feel a bit

melancholy. Boys never showed her much interest in school. She didn't know if it was because they considered her weird because she was an orphan or if it was because she wasn't interesting enough to them. As a foster child, she was never given any of the trendy clothing or other things kids her age had. She didn't even have a cell phone. Of course, being where she was now, the idea of having one seemed ridiculous. She doubted she could even get any reception if she had a phone with her.

Dmitri cleared his throat, ending her mental tirade. "I don't know about you, but the silence is kind of getting to me."

Mirielle shrugged. She'd enjoy being able to have a conversation, but once again, she was denied the ability, now having been reduced to communicating with gestures.

"I'd think I'd be used to it by now. I mean, I had my crew, but we didn't talk much outside of what was necessary. It was mainly concerning the *Mermaid Princess*. She was mine, and they worked for me. It was a simple relationship. Now, she's gone and I don't know if any of them survived." He shook his head, then gave her a sad smile. "At least I saved you."

An abrupt meow made itself known from Pouncer, prompting a chuckle.

Dmitri gave the tabby a scratch under his furry chin. "You too, Pounce."

That acknowledgement made the kitten purr with satisfaction.

Mirielle however, wasn't sure of what to think about Dmitri's curious insistence on saving her as being the bright side to their situation. It wasn't like she could pay him. Maybe he had a chivalrous side? He was quite enraged when she had gotten hit, after all.

He studied her a moment, then after a long pause said, "It looks good—the comb I mean. In your hair. It's… nice."

She felt herself flush at the compliment. It was strange being around someone who seemed to think she was pretty. She toyed with her platinum blonde hair, as she considered whether Dmitri was being truthful or just trying to fill in the sounds of birdsong and leaves rustling in the breeze with words.

"I'm still quite sure that the men who attacked us were pirates, which means they may have a ship somewhere… unless they got shipwrecked too. Either way, I'm going to get us out of here," Dmitri said, changing the subject. "I hope they don't have other crew members wandering about or waiting on their ship if they still have it. I prefer my ship, but since she's gone I'll take what I can get as long as it gets us to where we need to go."

Mirielle nodded, to show that she was listening since she couldn't think of any other reply to give him. She still couldn't help, but feel bad that he had lost his ship. It seemed to have meant a lot to him.

"I'm not boring you, am I?"

She shook her head.

"Good. Just trying to break up the monotony. I was never one for wandering in the woods. Not a big fan of nature unless it had to do with the sea. I grew up in a seaside-" he cut himself off then rubbed at his scruffy face. "That's not really important. It would just bore you to sleep. Then I'd have to carry both you and the furball. Which I wouldn't mind unless we were attacked, then we'd all be in trouble. And now I'm babbling. Great. So much for the etiquette lessons."

The last comment made Mirielle's eyebrows wing up. Why would a guy need etiquette lessons? Was he from a noble family? She could recall stories where children were instructed on everything from table manners to how to greet guests. She supposed it wasn't too farfetched that Dmitri might be the son of a nobleman. It was still surprising though.

Her thoughts were interrupted by her stomach growling. She gave Dmitri a bashful look that made him chuckle.

"You're adorable." He dug into his coat, taking out the bread and dried meat he had looted off the dead men. "I guess a snack won't hurt. We'll need to find water soon though. I don't want you getting dehydrate."

Mirielle nodded, mouthing a thank you as he held out some food to her.

"Just let me know if you need to stop. I'm guessing you aren't too used to walking so much," he said between mouthfuls of bread.

Mirielle sampled what she dubbed fish jerky and decided that it wasn't too bad. A little saltier than she would have liked, but food was food. Pouncer on the other hand was quite satisfied as Dmitri held out pieces to the feline. She let out a silent laugh at his prancing, then the joy melted away. Her face fell at the lack of sound making her feel hollow inside.

Dmitri noticed the sudden change as he looked at the blonde girl in concern. He put a hand on her shoulder, turning her to face him. "We'll get your voice back. Don't worry. I'm not going to let you down. I'll also keep the more unsavory types away from you. We'll get through this, I promise."

She gave a less than energetic nod. She wanted to believe him, but the longer she went without her voice, the more helpless she felt. Still, she refused to give up just yet.

He lifted her chin up, gazing deeply into her eyes as he repeated, "I *promise*."

Before Mirielle could react to the soulful look he gave her, Dmitri let her go, and began walking again leaving her staring after him befuddled. *Is he trying to tell me something or am I just imagining it.*

At a loss for an answer, she hurried after him.

Chapter 17

*M*irielle never thought she'd be so relieved to see the ocean again until that moment. It may not be drinking water, but docked along the shore was a ship with black sails. She guessed the men who had attacked them earlier had come from the vessel. It was surprising to see that it appeared to have not taken any damage from the storm that had ravaged the *Mermaid Princess.* It was also a lot smaller, to her amazement. She didn't know much about ships, but it was evident that this particular boat was less superior to that of the *Mermaid Princess.*

Dmitri grinned as he gave the vessel a thorough study. "Doesn't look inhabited from here, but we can't be too careful. Weapons out, we aren't taking any chances."

His female companion drew a deep breath as she unsheathed her rapier while his feline one ducked further into his clothing.

The captain brandished his cutlass and smirked. "Somehow, I think I might enjoy this. I've never commandeered a ship before. Plus I have to admit, they deserve it, despite her not looking like much. As long as she's sea worthy, that's all that matters. Everything else is just details."

A smile crept over Mirielle's lips. She couldn't argue with him even if she had her voice. It was also

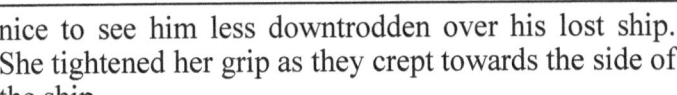
nice to see him less downtrodden over his lost ship. She tightened her grip as they crept towards the side of the ship.

Dmitri snorted as he pointed to the makeshift ramp leading onboard. "The fools left the plank. Their idiocy is our gain."

Mirielle nodded, she hoped there was no one left on the ship. Even armed she still felt vulnerable. She just wasn't used to fighting. It didn't mean she would not try, however. She'd do everything in her power to make sure they all survived, because that's just what you did—you took care of your team. She, Dmitri, and Pouncer were that team as few as they were. At least, that was the best label she could muster in her head.

"Stay close and if things get bad; run. Don't wait for me. Run, as fast as your legs will carry you," Dmitri added.

His only response was a sharp nod despite how much his blonde companion wanted to disagree. Now was not the time to argue. Especially, since she couldn't vocalize the way she wanted to. She'd just have to make him believe that was what she'd do to appease him. There was no way she'd leave him to die. Not after everything he had done for her.

She stayed light on her feet, preparing for Dmitri to give the signal to board the ship.

Green eyes focused on the stillness of the vessel, monitoring for any movement. Satisfied at still sighting none, he crept forward, beckoning Mirielle to follow suit. It wasn't long before they made it on board, and that was when everything went to pure chaos.

Chapter 18

If Mirielle still had her voice, she would have screamed, there was no doubt about it. No sooner had she and Dmitri entered the ship, several armed men leaped out of the shadows with their swords positioned for the kill.

Dmitri once again used himself to shield his companion. He gave the crew the most charming smile he could manage. "Greetings! We're lost and were just checking to see if this fine vessel was abandoned or not. We weren't looking to steal it, or anything!"

Mirielle could only bob her head in agreement.

"Then why are you armed?" A muscular man who sounded less than convinced inquired.

"Have you seen the world we live in? If it's not sea monsters, its bandits... not like you fine, upstanding citizens..." Dmitri let out a nervous chuckle. "Listen, I think we will leave now. Places to go, people to see..."

Mirielle plastered on a smile, but pondered if Dmitri was acting, or if he was as nervous as he sounded. Either way, it seemed to be backfiring because their opposition did not lower their weapons. Instead they came closer. *This isn't good. Not good at all.*

The two trespassers' blood went cold when they

heard a single sentence from a short man towards the back.

"Hey, isn't that Ivan's whip?" The stocky man gestured to the weapon still wrapped around Mirielle's belt.

The rest of the crew looked, and they went from cautious to murderous. Now it was going to get ugly.

Mirielle felt sweat sliding down her back as her fear grew stronger. She watched Dmitri, hoping he'd come up with a brilliant plan to save their necks.

Just as the men were about to attack a huge, monstrous wave appeared out of nowhere and crashed down, assaulting the ship. The pirates cried out as they were claimed by the water, yanking them out to sea. Just before it could reach the two shipwrecked companions, Dmitri grabbed Mirielle by the arm, forcing her to jump with him overboard, onto the thick sand. Once they reached the ground, he scrambled to his feet, pulling her along behind him as they sprinted towards the trees. The water reached for them, hindering their escape as it made their feet sink deeper into the sand with each step. Their efforts seemed futile as they struggled to keep moving.

Please, this can't be happening! I don't want to die like this. I refuse to! As another wave towered over them, Mirielle gripped at Dmitri's hand, squeezing her eyes shut. She wished there were a way to save them both. A warm feeling flooded her, but was snuffed out as a jarring laughter flooded her ears. Her eyes flew open and she gaped in shock at the wave. Encased in the water was a woman with flowing ebony hair that resembled sea weed, two fish tails for her lower extremities, and a bodice encrusted with what looked like crushed albacore. The woman sneered at Mirielle, sending shivers down her spine.

"Well, well, look who we've got here. The dear

little mermaid and her prince... or is he? You do realize dear, that to get your pretty voice back, you'll have to kill him. Such a pity, really," she cooed, examining her razor sharp fingernails.

Dmitri stared in shock at the sea creature. It took a moment for him to register what it was that she was saying. "What are you talking about? That has to be a lie!"

"Aww, did I just drive a wedge in your relationship? I'm not sorry," she snorted, flipping her hair. "Just keep in mind, you will never defeat me, you insignificant shrimp."

Mirielle scowled as she pondered why this woman insisted on mocking her and making threats. It didn't make any sense... until she thought back to the fairytale. If she was supposed to be the Little Mermaid then that meant this woman must be the sea witch. *Then did that make Dmitri a prince? Stop it, focus.*

"I am looking forward to using your foam in my next spell, dear."

Blue eyes flashed, as Mirielle drew her gaze back to the witch then with a snap of her wrist, cracked the whip at the wave which broke apart like shards of glass. The woman's cruel cackle seemed to echo around them before it faded.

Dmitri fell on his rear as the sand let up. He glanced up at Mirielle then shook his head. "I guess there's a lot of stuff we haven't been telling each other."

She gave him a sad smile, as she joined him on the sand, her mind still reeling over the potential of fairy tales being true. *And you're in one.*

Chapter 19

Mirielle for once, was glad she had lost her voice. It made it easier to avoid confusing Dmitri with her strange speculations. Instead she sat on the ground feeling awkward as she toyed with the whip in her hands. She felt his eyes on her, but didn't know how to respond. She pondered if the feeling was mutual.

"I guess there is more to you than I anticipated," he began, rubbing at his face. "Got tangled up with a sea witch I take it?"

His reply was a shrug. It didn't help that Mirielle had no idea of what was going on. She wasn't from that world, or so she thought. If only she could talk! She had so many questions building up in her that if she didn't get them out soon, she might explode.

She sighed, wishing there was an easy solution to her predicament. All she knew was that she had to find the Crystal Garden, yet she didn't know how to get there or where it was for that matter. She might as well have lost her vision too considering how lost she felt. She wished she could find someone who could help that knew of the things she had questions to. Until she was hit with such luck, she'd continue her aimless wandering with Dmitri.

"We should head out again. I doubt the boat is still there, but it won't hurt to look," her companion said, climbing to his feet. He paused to offer her his hands.

Mirielle looked at them, surprised that he wasn't trying to avoid her then accepted the help up. She gave him an appreciative smile then tucked the whip away.

They walked together in silence, even Pouncer stayed quiet perched on Dmitri's shoulder. Mirielle wished she was able to tell Dmitri what she knew in order to clear up whatever questions concerning her that were swarming his mind. She was still trying to put together the pieces, but there was little to go by.

"I don't know how much of what she said regarding you was true, but until I hear otherwise, I will not believe a word of it."

She looked at Dmitri, surprised by the earnest tone in his voice. There was so much she wanted to ask him, yet couldn't. Until she regained her voice, she would never be granted the answers she so wished to hear. Instead she was just his mute companion.

"I suspect that you have some form of amnesia, am I right?" He inquired, as they wound their way around a couple of trees, his green eyes staring off into the distance.

Mirielle shrugged when he glanced at her.

"You don't know?"

She nodded.

"Then I'll take that for a yes. I will admit, I was unsure when we first ran into each other, but after the encounter with the Sea Witch, I'm pretty certain that we have met before. In fact… you mistook my brother for me."

Chapter 20

Blue eyes widened as the confession left Dmitri's lips. She stared at him until he looked away, scratching at the back of his head. After a moment he released a sigh. "There's a reason why the mermaid on my ship resembled you. It's because we had met before, but it was brief. I was on my first ship, the one before the *Mermaid Princess*. I was arrogant and thought I could handle the monstrous storm that was brewing. I figured the sea was my destiny, not... my brother's life. So I sailed off despite everyone's protests. I didn't want to be confined to a life where I was a mere shadow."

Mirielle nodded, indicating that she was listening. He met her eyes for a moment then continued.

"It was fine at first, thrilling even. Then I was proven wrong. Between the wind and waves of the storm, my ship was ripped apart and I knew it was only time before death would claim me for my stupidity. I blacked out as the sea devoured my vessel. The only thing I remember after that is lying on the beach with someone who resembled you looking down upon me. There was a whisper of a song left in the air before my rescuer vanished." Dmitri came to a halt then took Mirielle's hands in his. "I don't know if it was you or not, but I still want to say, thank you. Perhaps when you get your voice back, your memories will follow. Until then, I will continue to aid you in your quest for as long as you need me."

Mirielle felt her heart flutter at the renewed promise. After the encounter with the sea witch she was afraid that it was just a matter of time before he realized that helping a mute stranger wasn't worth the effort. To hear otherwise, she couldn't help but give him a joyful smile.

Dmitri's face redden at her reaction. He cleared his throat, dropping one hand as he pulled her along with the other. "We should keep moving. The sooner we figure out where we are, the sooner we can see about breaking the curse."

Curse? What curse? Mirielle jerked back, stunned by the words. This was the first time she had ever heard of such a thing.

"Sorry, I guess you don't know or maybe 'don't remember' is the more accurate term." He winced, shifting his feet. "This place, including the kingdom will be swallowed by the sea unless we can get the curse broken before the end of the mermaid princess's sixteenth birthday. And that, if the prophecy is accurate, is today."

Chapter 21

$\mathcal{M}$irielle didn't know what to think. First she was the Little Mermaid from the stories and now there was a curse involved, which a prophecy states she is supposed to break today! Plus it was her birthday! Was it really? She thought back to the last time she had seen anything indicating what the date was. Two days ago it was July 19th so it was now... July 22nd, the day written in her files as a possible birthday. She never bothered to mention it to anyone because the likelihood that the agency's guess was right seemed ludicrous. However, to have some sort of confirmation... *Could that be right?*

As a child who didn't even know who her parents were, Mirielle was never certain when her birthday was. However, if she was indeed the mermaid princess, then she would know at last. For a strange reason, she felt a bit of happiness over the news despite the ugliness of having to deal with a curse. She'd know for sure when her birthday was. Plus she was indeed sixteen.

"Mir? Are you all right? You have a strange look on your face..."

The blonde haired girl blinked and blushed at having spaced out. She nodded then twisted her hair around, hoping her face didn't turn too bright a shade of red.

Dmitri chuckled. "Sorry, didn't mean to embarrass you."

She continued tangling her fingers in her pale blonde locks, unsure of what to do. If she could talk, she might say something off the wall to get the attention off herself and onto whatever topic she brought up. Instead she had to remain looking awkward. Her eyes widened at the squeeze of her hand that she had forgotten was still holding Dmitri's.

"It's okay. I'm sure there's a lot you'd share if you could, but all you can do is just think it since you still don't have your voice. When you do get it back, I will be eager to listen if you wish to share."

Mirielle nodded. There was just something about Dmitri that put her at ease. The thought of being able to tell him about whatever happened to be on her mind, made her warm inside. She didn't think she could have asked for a better companion. Since he had stuck with her so far, she decided that he would be the first person she would share those thoughts with.

They continued journeying through the forest until they came across what looked like a hut. Dmitri's brows knit together at the sight of the little ramshackle structure. It appeared as though it would collapse like a house of cards if a strong breeze were to come by. The two travelers exchanged glances, pondering if they should peek inside or continue on. There was a chance that there might be someone inside that could aid them, yet another possibility that they could be dangerous. It was a risk either way.

"What do you think? Should we?" Dmitri inquired, looking at the girl at his side.

Mirielle studied the building. Her stomach churned with an uneasiness that centered on the fact that they did not know what hid beyond the makeshift door if anything. The possibilities seemed endless, igniting

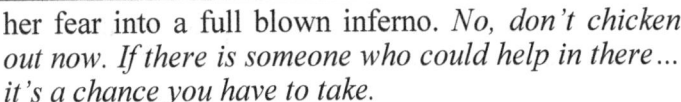

her fear into a full blown inferno. *No, don't chicken out now. If there is someone who could help in there… it's a chance you have to take.*

She squared her shoulders then unsheathed her rapier, not wanting to be at a disadvantage if they ran into trouble.

Dmitri did the same with his cutlass, "I guess this means we're going in."

Mirielle bobbed her head. Her nerves knotted up her stomach even tighter with each cautious step they made. She wanted to change her mind and skip investigating the hut all together, but that was the coward's way out. She had to know who or what was inside.

After a hesitant moment, the two companions stood outside the entrance, then stepped through the threshold. To say it was not what they expected was an understatement. Sheets of parchment littered the ground. A pile of dirty, thread worn blankets were bundled up in a corner. On the opposite side were several tattered tomes, their leather covers stained and in shambles. What they did not see, however, was a single person or creature.

"Odd. It doesn't look like anyone has been here for a long time, yet they left their things behind," Dmitri scowled, taking in all the junk spread about. "I wonder what happened to them."

Mirielle pursed her lips. She was tempted to peruse the books and papers. There might be something useful to them, maybe even directions to the Crystal Garden or a way to break the curse.

She bent down, reaching out for a rather dusty tome when a loud crackle of lightning made her jump with a soundless shriek.

"Who goes there? Who has the audacity to enter my home?" A gravelly voice echoed all around them.

Dmitri moved in close to Mirielle, "I think we might have a problem…"

Chapter 22

"*I* asked you a question. You owe me an answer!" the voice ordered as another bolt of lightning illuminated the small room.

Mirielle flinched, her fear rising like a tidal wave as she and Dmitri remained blind to whose ever home they had intruded.

Dmitri's grip on her tightened as Pouncer cowered in his collar. "We don't mean any harm. The place looked abandoned so we-"

"So you thought you could take whatever it was you wished!" Thunder boomed as the ground shook.

"No! We were hoping to find some information on the curse or the Crystal Garden or even where we might be. We got shipwrecked." The captain explained, staying close to his blonde companion.

The storm that seemed to surround them died off. A small figure stepped into the hut, wearing a multi-colored cloak in shades of blues, greens and golds. He also had a long white beard, and rope sandals. "Greetings and salutations!"

Dmitri's jaw dropped at the sight of the man who was no taller than three feet high. It was obvious that the little man was not what was expected. "Greetings…"

Mirielle gave an apologetic smile in hopes that the stranger would not be too angry with them.

"So you were telling the truth after all. Good for you," the man walked to Mirielle then took her hands as he studied her face. "You really are the princess. Perhaps we are not doomed after all."

Deep blue eyes fluttered at the word 'princess.' Acknowledging that she was the Little Mermaid was enough, but being a princess as well—it was quite a lot to take in. Still, she didn't shy away from the stranger.

He then turned to face the dark haired captain, rubbing at his beard. "I have to admit, I am quite surprised to see you here, Prince Dmitri."

Mirielle gaped in shock at her companion. He never mentioned that he was royalty.

"Right. Well, I guess the cat is out of the bag…" The prince began, which prompted Pouncer to pop his head out of his hiding spot with an expectant look on his furry face. "Not you."

"Oh dear," the elderly man began. "I believe I must have said something I shouldn't have. My apologies, Your Highness."

Dmitri's brows knit together, but he didn't bother correcting the man. "May we at least have your name since you seem to know so much about us already?"

"Of course. It is Fenton."

"Wait! I know you. You used to work at the castle as an advisor."

Fenton chuckled, "Very good. I'm glad to hear that I have not been forgotten after all."

"Why are you here?" Dmitri inquired, confusion now flooding his face. "You just up and left one day if what I heard was correct."

The little man picked through the scrolls still scattered on the ground. "I suppose you could say that I had a higher calling."

"What are you talking about?"

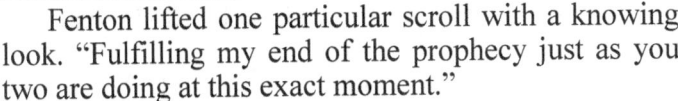

Fenton lifted one particular scroll with a knowing look. "Fulfilling my end of the prophecy just as you two are doing at this exact moment."

Mirielle and Dmitri exchanged silent glances. The more the prophecy was mentioned, the more urgent it was to find out what it said about them.

"Why don't we have a bit of tea and some of the biscuits I brought, then we shall discuss everything you need to know..." He gestured to what once was a pile of books, which somehow had reverted to that of a table and chairs.

Is he like some sort of wizard or something? Mirielle pondered while she took a seat. The longer she was in this strange world, the more it felt like a dream. Yet, for some reason, a part of her knew it was far more than just a figment of her imagination.

Fenton unearthed a large cloth covered plate and a teapot from a basket. He retrieved three cups, poured in a flowery scented tea into each one. He set each one down in front of his guests, leaving one for himself. With a snap of his wrist he removed the napkin, unveiling stacks of fresh biscuits. "Please, don't be shy, help yourselves."

"Thank you," Dmitri replied, then offered Mirielle one of the biscuits. He smiled as she accepted. The prince's green eyes widened when Fenton set a bowl of water and some fresh smoked fish down on the floor. Pouncer took notice as well, scampering from his haven then dove towards his treat.

The old man chuckled. "It's only fair for your feline friend to partake in a meal as well."

"I'm sure he thanks you too," Dmitri nodded to the purring kitten. "So what can you tell us about the prophecy?"

"Eat, first. You'll need all the strength you can get."

Mirielle paused mid-bite. She lifted her gaze to Fenton's then mimed writing.

"Yes, dear. I will find you a quill and blank parchment, but first you must eat." He nodded, waving his hands in a shooing motion. He took a sip of tea and began, "It's obvious that you have lost your memories so I shall tell you what I know…"

Chapter 23

*M*irielle leaned forward in her seat, waiting with anticipation for Fenton to continue. She wasn't sure why she was so intrigued, but if there was any truth to the old man's words, she was eager to listen.

"According to the prophecy, if by the end of the mermaid princess's sixteenth birthday, the curse has not been broken, then the entire kingdom of Oceanvale shall be consumed by the sea." Fenton explained between a bite of food.

Dmitri winced. "Is there any information on how to prevent it? I mean, I don't know about you, but I'd prefer not having to have a mass exodus to another kingdom."

"Just the power of the mermaid princess's Crystal Rose. There is no further information including the location of the rose itself. All that is stated is that the mermaid princess is the only one that can break the curse."

"That's real helpful," the prince grumbled, as he bit into a biscuit. "Didn't you mention me being in their earlier?"

Fenton raised an eyebrow at the younger man's lack of table manners. "I see you have already forgotten about your etiquette…"

Dmitri shrugged then said around a mouthful of

food. "It's not needed on a ship."

"You are still royalty."

"It doesn't matter."

The old man shook his head in disapproval. "You cannot behave that way in court. Your parents-"

The prince rolled his eyes then launched to his feet. "I'm never going to be king, so what is the point? I'll always be the unnecessary twin brother of the son who is next in line for the throne!"

"You don't know that!" Fenton argued, raising his voice.

Mirielle stared in horror at the exchange. She had never seen Dmitri look so distraught before. It was like seeing a whole other side of him that he tried to conceal. She wanted to give him some reassuring words, but her lack of voice prevented her. She tried to touch his arm, but he moved away.

"Yes, I do! Nicholai is the one the kingdom needs. Not me. I am insignificant while he gets everything he desires. I am tired of being nothing more than his worthless clone. I gave up everything to find my own path only to have it sunk!" Dmitri shoved his hands through his dark hair in frustration. "You know what? This is all pointless. No one needs me. Nicholai is better suited for saving the world anyway. I'm out of here."

Before either Fenton or Mirielle could react, Dmitri stormed out of the little hut without a second glance back.

Chapter 24

What just happened? Mirielle stared at the doorway pondering whether she should go after Dmitri, or leave him alone. It wasn't like she was able to say anything to him. She stared hard at her tea, wishing it could give her some sort of advice on what to do.

Pouncer looked up at her with wide green eyes, begging for her to bring back his human companion.

Mirielle sighed and scratched behind his ears for a moment. She gave Fenton a smile who made a waving motion towards the door. She rose to her feet and left the safe confinements of the hut.

Where did he go? She made a face at the trees which surrounded her, but saw no sign of the upset prince. Mirielle wasn't even sure what she'd do when she found him. If she could talk, she'd tell him about her life and that she understood how it felt to be unnecessary. Then again, she didn't know if what she thought was her life was real or not. How could she be an orphan on the swim team if she was also supposed to be the mermaid princess? It didn't make sense.

She also didn't like the idea of just wandering around aimlessly in search of Dmitri, but she didn't want him to be alone either. With her mind made up, she headed off in one direction, hoping that it was the right one.

It didn't take Mirielle too long to catch a glimpse of Dmitri stalking a short ways ahead of her. His pace was brisk, and she wasn't sure if she should leave him be or not. Mirielle drew a deep breath and jogged towards him.

He turned his head, giving her a single glance then continued on his way. "You're better off with my brother. Everyone is."

I don't even know your brother. She frowned then realizing that he wasn't going to stop, grabbed his hand.

"What?" Dmitri spun around and faced the blonde haired girl. His green eyes sparked with fury. "I told you, I'm not the one who should be helping you. I'm nobody. An afterthought. Go find Nicholai. I'm sure he'll be better suited to helping you with your quest than me."

Mirielle shook her head. She wished she was able to speak so she could try to talk some sense into him.

"Go!" He snatched his hand out of her grasp.

She stared at him as he stepped back from her so she did the only thing she could, she threw her arms around him in a hug.

Dmitri froze, he gaped at the girl wrapped around him in shock. "Mir…"

Mirielle tightened her hold, not wanting to give him the chance to push her away. She refused to let go, not until he agreed to continue helping her. When she got her voice back, she'd work on showing him that he had more meaning than he assumed. Instead she'd just try her best to convince him that she wasn't going anywhere without him.

He released a heavy sigh as his head drooped over hers. "You're not going to take no for an answer, are you…"

The blonde shook her head against his chest. She

would dig in her heels and be dragged if that's what it took to stop Dmitri from leaving. She didn't want to travel with his brother. After all, Dmitri was the one who stated he'd help her and she was determined to make him keep his word.

"I don't know what you are thinking, but… thanks." Dmitri hugged Mirielle back, his face coloring in a slight blush. "I guess that this might be an attempt to make me continue on this adventure with you. Okay, you win."

Mirielle stepped back, giving him a grateful smile. She was relieved that despite being unable to talk, that she was still able to communicate with Dmitri.

"Well, let's get back to Fenton. Maybe he can give us a clue as to where to look next."

She nodded, then turned to head back the way they came when a particular smell caught her attention.

Dmitri stiffened by her side. "Is that smoke? We better hurry!"

Together they raced towards the hut, fearing the worse.

Chapter 25

*N*o! Mirielle cried in silence. They were too late.

Hot flames were consuming what was left of the hut as it collapsed into shambles. Dmitri tried to go inside, but the heat was too much. Mirielle ran towards him then slid on something that almost made her lose her footing. She barely had a chance to catch herself to keep from falling backwards. She shifted her gaze downward and choked at the sight of the bloody pool she was standing in.

"No, no, no… No!" Dmitri pulled her away from the crimson liquid, shuddering at the sight of Fenton's charred hand lying inches away. The old man had been murdered. "We have to go. We have to get out of here!"

A rustling from behind the pair made them freeze in fear. Mirielle risked a glance over her shoulder then breathed a sigh of relief at the sight of the terrified orange tabby bounding towards them. Pouncer leaped into her arms, shaking with fear.

"You're okay, Pounce. I'm just glad to see that you got away from whoever did this." The prince stroked the cat with comforting hands. He looked into Mirielle's blue eyes, his expression grave. "We better run. It's not safe here. I know, I'm stating the obvious, but let's just get out of here."

Mirielle gave him a nod. She didn't want to face whoever had killed Fenton. A part of her was furious—they had not only stolen an innocent man's life, but also her sole source for answers concerning the curse and the Crystal Garden. Now everything that could have been used for information had gone up in smoke, including paper she could have used for communicating with. It was all such a horrible waste.

Dmitri kept a hand on her arm, his other on his cutlass as he sped through the clusters of trees. The pair wove around the dense foliage, desperate to find some place safe. He came to a dead halt as something that resembled a scream filled the air. He pulled Mirielle down with him, holding her close as they tried to determine where the sound was coming from.

This is not in the story... Mirielle thought in bitterness over her predicament. It was lame, but seemed to loosen up some of the fear that was trying to choking her. Did Fenton die because of her? The possibility seemed plausible given she was supposed to break a curse. Did that mean more people would die? What will happen to Dmitri? Would he meet the same fate?

Just the thought of the prince's death made her eyes sting. She couldn't let that happen. There had to be another way. She settled her hand into his. Feeling his fingers wrap around her own, she tightened her grip. Pouncer chose that moment to duck back under the young man's collar.

Dmitri leaned close to Mirielle's ear as he whispered, "I think whatever that was—it is gone. We should move again."

She shook her head.

"Mir. We can't stay here. Whoever murdered Fenton might do the same to us."

The blonde haired girl's whimper remained

unheard, but Dmitri did catch her grimace.

"I'm not going to let them hurt you if it's the last thing I do, understand?"

Despite the reassuring words, Mirielle didn't feel any better. If anything, she felt worse. She didn't want Dmitri to put his life on the line for her. She wasn't sure what she felt for him, but knew his death was the last thing she wanted in the world.

Dmitri tried pulling her to her feet. Despite her resistance, she gave in. It was a short matter of time before they were running again.

Chapter 26

Mirielle raced through the woods alongside Dmitri as fast as her legs could carry her. It wasn't long before she had to stop—running was a lot different from swimming despite her physical fitness. She was grateful that the only affliction from the story she read of *The Little Mermaid* was losing her voice and not the pain the poor girl experienced each time she took a step.

If I had to go through that, Dmitri would have to carry me. The thought of being curled up in his strong arms made her face heat up. She had no doubt that he was capable, she just didn't like the idea of being a burden. It was bad enough being unable to talk. At least she was still able to pull her own weight.

"Is that... water?" The prince's pace increased as he almost let out a cheer. Mirielle did her best to keep up with him, despite the fact that he was still holding her hand.

When they came to a halt on the beach, Dmitri's eyes seemed to sparkle with pure joy. Mirielle couldn't help but smile at his blissful expression.

"Maybe we can find some driftwood or even a boat!" The excitement died down in his eyes as a splintered piece of wood washed ashore. It looked like it came from the wreckage of a boat. "Unless that sea witch gets us first."

The bitterness of Dmitri's words caught his female companion's attention. She winced as he gave the wood a swift kick back into the water. If only there was something she could do to better their situation. She knelt on the beach then wrote in the sand, 'We'll figure it out. Don't give up hope.'

He looked at her then nodded. "You're right. Thanks."

Mirielle gave him a small smile, relieved that she was able to help in some way.

They walked along the beach. The sound of seagulls cawing in the distance mingling with the ocean waves brought an odd sense of peace. It was not to be trusted. Not with potential danger out there, threatening their lives.

Dmitri took her hand again, but said nothing as he did so. It was obvious that there was a lot on his mind and even though he didn't want to share his thoughts, he didn't want to abandon Mirielle either. She threaded her fingers with his, which made him pause in mid-step in surprise. She gave him a small smile then they continued walking.

"You know, that comb really does look great in your hair. Almost like it's always been meant for you," he commented, glancing at her from the corner of his eye.

Mirielle blushed and mouthed the word thank you. She felt happy in this moment. Deep down a fear stirred in her belly. What if Dmitri decides that she's not worth the effort anymore? What if he leaves her to fend for herself or dumps her on the next helpful stranger they come across? Maybe that was his plan when he left her with Fenton.

The thought sent ice down her spine as a voice that sounded like her own chimed in her mind. "*It's only a matter of time before he ditches you just like everyone else does. Who are you even kidding that he cares about what happens to you? It's all lies. You don't matter in this world, just like you didn't matter in your own. You are nothing to anyone. Isolation is your sole destiny."*

The blonde was unaware of her own tears until Dmitri came to an abrupt halt.

He gazed at her, his eyes filled with concern as he dropped her hand and touched her shoulder. "Are you all right?"

Mirielle's eyes reminded fixed, staring straight ahead as though she couldn't see him. She gave no sign that she even heard him. It was like being stuck behind a sheet of glass, she could see everything going on, but couldn't move. The harsh words in her head seemed to drown everything out. She wanted to scream at it to stop, but still lacked a voice.

"Mir!" Dmitri knelt in front of her and shook her arms. Still nothing. His breath caught in his throat at her frozen expression. He patted her face with a shaky hand, but she didn't react. "Mirielle! Snap out of it and tell me what's wrong!"

Pouncer popped out of his collar then padded over and tried licking at her face. He turned to the panicked prince, meowing at him.

"I-I don't know, Pounce. I don't know what to do…" He stared at the catatonic girl for a long moment then made up his mind. In one quick movement he pulled her to him, as he pressed him lips against hers.

Mirielle blinked in shock, the cruel voices in her head were silenced as Dmitri's last ditch effort to break her free worked its magic. She let out a gasp of surprise, unsure of what to do. She had never kissed anyone before and was quite stunned that the prince decided to use such a tactic to bring her back.

He must have felt her stiffen because he released her before she could even think of returning the kiss. His face was flushed as he cast his gaze down to the sand for a moment before meeting her blue eyes in concern. "Sorry, I wasn't sure what to do. You were out of it- are you all right?"

She bit her lip, feeling a little disappoint over him having pulled away, but nodded.

Dmitri rubbed at his chin then moved his hand to the back of his neck. He looked very awkward and unsure as he shifted from foot to foot. "Good. I'm glad. I- We should keep moving."

He took her hand, pulling her along before she could come up with anything to write in the sand. Mirielle chewed on her lip, wondering if there was more to the kiss, or if the voice was right and she was just kidding herself. After all, she had been discarded her whole life. Why should it be any different now?

Chapter 27

What happened to me? Mirielle couldn't help, but shake the feeling that there was more wrong with her than just her lost voice. The fact that she couldn't move until Dmitri had kissed her was quite alarming.

Her disturbed thoughts shifted to a different one that brought heat to her face. He had kissed her. Not only that, it was her first kiss. She wished she knew what it meant, if anything. Blue eyes shifted up to the prince, but he didn't look at her. His hand remained around hers, but it felt different, almost as though he were unsure of what he was doing. It made Mirielle confused and a little guilty for some reason. It was an odd emotion to feel, but there it was.

She released a silent sigh. As if things couldn't get any more complicated, she found herself proven wrong. Now, she didn't know what to do when it came to Dmitri. It didn't help that he seemed even more awkward around her than before.

Pouncer peered up at Dmitri with an inquisitive meow. The prince said nothing even when the kitten licked at his face.

Mirielle gave Pouncer an apologetic look. She knew it was her fault that the feline's human companion's mood had changed. She wished she knew how to fix it. *Of course, not being able to talk is a huge disadvantage in that.*

The frustrated part of her wanted to run out to the ocean and call out to the sea witch just to get the inevitable over with. Her fear and lack of voice hindered that plan. So instead, she was stuck only being able to wander around with Dmitri in hopes of finding some sort of clue on how to destroy the curse or get to the Crystal Garden.

Her stomach twisted up into knots when she glanced up at him again. Weren't kisses supposed to bring people closer together? Was everything she had read in books or seen in movies wrong? Now, it felt like he was miles away from her. *He probably doesn't care about me. After all, no one ever has. Either that or he's disgusted by me and is too polite to say it. Rather than torture him further with my presence, I should just leave.*

After a few more steps, Mirielle yanked her hand away from Dmitri's. He came to a halt, his expression almost startled as she drew back. "What's wrong?"

Mirielle clenched her hands into fists wishing she could express her thoughts with words. Instead she shook her head as her eyes stung with unshed tears.

"Mirielle, what is it?" He reached for her, but she evaded. Dmitri frowned, concern etched over his face. "Are you all right? Do you need to stop? We can take a break if you want."

She continued to shake her head, despising the fact that she still couldn't talk. Instead she continued walking backwards. *Stop pretending. You don't care about me. No one does. Just stop lying!*

Dmitri tried to grab her shoulders, but she slapped his hands away. Before he could think of anything to say, she turned on her heel and ran.

Chapter 28

Salty tears flooded her vision as Mirielle's feet pounded against the coarse sand. What in the world was she doing? She was used to being discarded so why did the idea of Dmitri not caring about her feel life a knife to her gut? Even worse, why was she running? Everything in her head was so messed up that she couldn't seem to make sense of anything. Now it all seemed like nothing more than irrational foolishness.

Stupid. I'm such an idiot! If I don't get control over myself then what help am I going to be in breaking the stupid curse? Then again, why do I even care? This isn't my world. At least, I don't think it is. Mirielle plopped down on the ground, landing on her hands and knees. She grasped at fistfuls of sand, trying in desperation to make sense of things.

She was supposed to find the Crystal Garden and break a curse. She also couldn't talk. Dmitri wanted to help her or so it seemed. He also had been keeping secrets from her, so she wasn't sure how well she could trust him anymore. Then there was the sea witch and whoever killed Fenton. Mirielle's conclusion— she was an idiot for parting ways with Dmitri. There were too many threats around, which meant she was in danger. Her best chance of survival was to find Dmitri.

The idea of returning to him with her tail between her legs after a silent outburst made Mirielle shudder. It was bad enough that she made herself look like an overemotional twit, now she'd have to face him again and hope that he wasn't going to treat her like the idiot she felt like. *Why do things have to be so complicated?*

Mirielle drew her knees to her chest, tucking her chin under them. She didn't know what to do. A part of her wanted to find Dmitri and continue the quest together, yet another part was afraid everything he had told her was nothing but a lie. She didn't want to be treated like she was nothing. Not anymore. It hurt too much to have no true value to others.

"No one is ever going to care about you. Your destiny is to always be alone. You have no worth. How can you even expect to break a curse in a world you have never been to until now? It'd be best to just give up. You are powerless to do anything."

Mirielle groaned, covering her ears as the voice that sounded so much like her own began berating her. She didn't want to listen, but the more she heard, the more she realized that it had a point. Who was she kidding? She was an unwanted orphan. Not even her swim team considered her a friend. She was just there. She doubted they even knew she was gone.

Tears streamed down her pale cheeks as she remained frozen with her forehead pressed to her knees. The blonde girl was so lost in her thoughts that she didn't see the wave rise above her then crash down, sweeping her out to sea.

Chapter 29

"Mirielle!" Her head snapped up. Her brows knit together as she found herself back in the strange white abyss that she had met the golden haired girl in. Mirielle just had to look over her shoulder to catch the stern gaze of a pair of violet eyes. It took a moment for the stranger's name to register in her head. *Lunette.*

The girl pressed a hand to her chest as she released a sigh of relief. "You're alert. Good, you had me scared for a minute. I wasn't sure what I was going to do if you didn't respond."

Mirielle shrugged her shoulders. It wasn't like she could communicate with Lunette. *This is all pointless.*

"No, it's not. I don't know what happened, but it seems as though your resolve has been wavering. Did something happen to make you so doubtful of yourself? Don't forget, this is in your head so you can still communicate with me."

The blue eyed blonde winced. Where should she begin? *Why was I chosen if I'm nothing?*

Lunette frowned. "What makes you feel as though you have no worth?"

Mirielle stared at her hard. How could she not see what everyone else seemed to all along? Was she that blind or naïve? *I'm not important. I never will be.*

"You're wrong! Look, I know all of this is

confusing, but you need to believe me when I tell you that whatever it is your mind is trying to tell you is nothing but lies. You are needed and Dmitri is the only one outside of the rest of us chosen by the Crystal Garden that can help you." Lunette grabbed her companion by the arms, forcing her to look at her. "Listen to your heart, not your head. There is apparently more to the spell you were put under than your lost voice. You can't give up now because that is what the witch wants you to do. Don't give in."

Mirielle bit her bottom lip as she felt her eyes begin to flood. She bowed her head, not wanting to be seen crying. *I just want to go home.*

"I know you won't believe me, but you are home. Please, hang in there. In the meantime, you have to fight whatever is trying to manipulate you. You are stronger than you think. Just believe in yourself. You are more important to the world than you could ever dream." Lunette's voice was soft as she tried to encourage the insecure girl. "You can do this."

Okay. Mirielle sniffled. She rubbed her eyes with the backs of her hands before lifting her head. *I still don't know what I'm supposed to do. Fenton and his scrolls were destroyed in a fire.*

"You will find your way. Don't worry. I wish I could tell you more, but you will be waking up soon. Remember, don't let your mind smother out your heart."

With those final words, Lunette disappeared from sight as Mirielle found herself engulfed by a whirlpool of water.

Chapter 30

With a silent gasp, Mirielle shot upright as her eyes flew open. She blinked several times in an attempt to clear her hazy vision then frowned. Where was she?

The last thing she could recall was sitting on the beach after having run away from Dmitri. Now she was sitting in what looked like a pile of lumber. Upon closer examination she realized that it was the remains of some sort of boat or ship.

Is this the Mermaid Princess? She bit her bottom lip as she pushed herself to her feet. There wasn't much left of whatever vessel it was, most of which would have to be reduced to kindling to be of any use. There wasn't anything remaining to indicate where the wood had come from. Mirielle guessed that the rest must be under the water. It saddened her to think of Dmitri's lost ship. He had taken the loss hard. Now she couldn't help, except to feel guilty over having left him.

Mirielle sighed as she glanced at the palm trees swaying in the gentle breeze. She had to find her way back to him, but how? She didn't even know where she was or how she got there. It was so frustrating how no matter what she did, she seemed to dig herself into a deeper hole.

Her hand brushed her waist. The rapier was still

there, but somehow she had lost the whip. At least she wasn't unarmed. She could find some gratitude for that. Still, the weapon provided little comfort. She would rather trade it for a map directing her to Dmitri. Now she was truly on her own, and to say she was even the least bit intimidated was an understatement.

Deal with it. You got yourself into this mess, you're going to have to get yourself out. Mirielle squared her shoulders in a desperate attempt to muster as much courage as she could. She wasn't used to being brave. She never had enough self-confidence to take the lead or make any decisions that would affect others. She was a follower. Just another cog in the system. Now however, she had to take care of herself and hold onto the hope that she would be able to find Dmitri.

She'd have to figure out some way to apologize to him. Knowing her luck, he was probably infuriated with her and had no desire to help her anymore. She couldn't let that possibility deter her. She did this to herself and would have to face the consequences no matter what they were.

With her head held high, Mirielle stepped through the wreckage. She had to fix things if it was the last thing she ever did. As she walked towards the trees, she let out a silent scream as her foot sank deeper into the sand. She gritted her teeth, yanking at it, but lost her balance, falling forward. Mirielle used her hands to try to catch herself, realizing too late that she had been caught by quick sand.

Fear bubbled up in her as she struggled to free herself. She knew no one could ever hear her. She was helpless to find any aid, sinking deeper by the minute. It wouldn't be too long before the sand consumed her.

So much for my apology! How in the world am I going to get out of this? Serves me right for being so stupid! She was going to die and there was no possible way to change her fate. Her last fleeting thought was of Dmitri before the sand swallowed her.

Chapter 31

*J*ust when Mirielle had thought she had met her end, the world seemed to shake around her. She opened her eyes to find herself sitting on what looked like a pedestal made of sand.

"Jump! I don't think I can hold you for too much longer!"

She didn't ask any questions as she did as she was told. When Mirielle landed on the soft sand, she found herself facing a girl with the longest hair she had ever seen standing a few feet away. By her side was an auburn haired man holding the reins of a beautiful gray stallion. Her companion studied the wreckage with an air of skepticism.

"Are you all right?" The brunette stranger asked, racing towards Mirielle. She gave the confused blonde a small smile. "I apologize. I didn't mean to startle you. My name is Cybele, and this is Tristan-"

He touched her arm. "Are you sure that's a good idea? We do not know who she is…"

Cybele shook her head, the skirt of her green gown bellowing in the wind. "I feel as though I know her, or at least of her. I think she is like me."

Mirielle blinked. Did that mean she knew of the Crystal Garden as well?

"I am glad I reached you in time. If I was a second later… It doesn't matter. What does is that you are free." The brunette let out a satisfied sigh. "I know you are looking for the Crystal Garden. The best advice I can tell you is to listen to your heart. It's the only key you need. Everything else should come together."

The blonde dropped to the ground then wrote in the sand, 'You know about the Crystal Garden?'

Tristan's brows knit together. "You're mute? I'm not judging, I was blind for a while after all."

Mirielle nodded. She decided not to take offense once she caught the earnest look the young man gave her. Somehow, she didn't believe he was lying. It also gave her renewed hope. If he could get his sight back then maybe she would find a way to get her voice to return.

"You are the Mermaid Princess," Cybele said with a knowing glint in her eyes. "That explains it."

I guess she's heard of the tale as well. Mirielle thought with a sensation of dejection. She didn't know how much truth was in the story, but the idea of dissolving into sea foam was not the least bit appealing. It was the one part that made her loath the fairy tale. She often chose to ignore it because it was a cruel ending.

"I wish I could be of more help, but all I can tell you is to continue your search for the Crystal Garden and once you have achieved your goals, to help us in locating Lunette. I'm sure she has already appeared to you. She's done so for the rest of us I believe. It's only polite to return the favor." Cybele patted Mirielle's hand. "You'll be fine. Just take faith in yourself."

Mirielle frowned then shook the girl's shoulder before returning to the sand. 'Have you seen a dark haired guy? He might have an orange kitten with him.'

"Back that way," Tristan pointed behind him. "He wasn't very talkative but did ask about a girl matching

your description."

She wrote 'Thank you!' with a big smiley face before taking off into the direction, leaving the couple to continue their personal journey on their own.

Chapter 32

*M*irielle had never run so fast before in her life. She was relieved that she had washed ashore the same place she and Dmitri had been originally shipwrecked. She hoped he wasn't too angry with her. The thought of him being furious with her made her eyes sting. She was so mixed up that she didn't know what she was doing anymore.

"That's because you are nothing, but a pathetic girl who should have never been born."

There was that voice again. It was hers, but not her words. At least she didn't think they were. Despite how much she didn't want to listen, they managed to cloud her thoughts enough that she wavered mid-step. Mirielle covered her ears, shaking her head to get it out. *No! I don't know where you came from, but that's not what I think...*

"Which is what a person in denial would say. Face it, you are too weak willed to do anything on your own. Who are you kidding? You can't break a curse let alone stand on your own two feet. You will not amount to anything."

Stop it! Mirielle inhaled deep before expelling the air from her lungs only to repeat the process several more times. She couldn't let the negativity control her. It's what got her into this mess to begin with. She wanted to scream at the top of her lungs for it to leave her alone, yet knew she couldn't utter a single sound. It was maddening how much she yearned to make the tiniest squeak in order to feel normal again.

Instead all the blonde could do was clench her teeth together and force her feet to move. Each step felt like sharp needles stabbing into the soles of her feet. Mirielle was surprised to see she wasn't leaving a bloody trail behind her given how much agony she felt, but continued to push onward. She had to make it back to Dmitri. She owed him that much after everything he had done for her.

Just when she felt like she couldn't go on any further, she collapsed. In frustration, Mirielle picked up a handful of sand and threw it. She didn't want to fail. Sure, she may not believe everything she was told, but that didn't mean she had to give up all together. She just wished she had some sort of clue as to where she had to go.

In defeat she stared down at the sand. Her feet felt as though the bottoms had been skinned then set on fire. Tears blurred her vision, but she refused to let them fall. She kept her focus on her hands, hoping that the pain would dissipate if she gave herself a small break. There was no telling how much further she'd have to go to find Dmitri.

Please give me the chance to at least apologize. Determination flashed in her blue eyes, as she lifted her head. If she couldn't walk, she'd crawl. She'd find her way back to him if it killed her.

Mirielle started forward, only to catch her skirt and collapsed back to the sandy ground. Wearing a dress would prove to be a challenge. She considered cutting the material to just above her knees, but wasn't certain how taboo it was to show off her legs in this particular world.

Shoving that thought aside she tried again and

achieved the same result. Gritting her teeth, Mirielle pushed herself to her knees then lifted the long skirt so it pooled around her. She unsheathed her rapier and made a long cut before hacking away at the material of the skirt until it was at the desired length. Satisfied with her crude handiwork, she put her rapier back then set about her journey, crawling with more ease than before.

It wasn't long before her hands and knees began to kill her. This was much easier in her head. Despite the extreme discomfort, she continued on until her arms shook and she felt as though she were about to kiss the sand.

"My, you are really putting up a fight... Too bad you shall never reach your precious prince."

Mirielle didn't even have to glance up to know that it was the sea witch mocking her. It wasn't like things were getting any better, now she had to deal with this... sea woman-creature-thing again. Couldn't anything ever go right for a change? Mirielle plopped down on the ground with a sigh, giving the witch a weary look. So much for achieving her goal.

"Look at me when I am talking to you, girl," the witch scolded.

The blonde sighed. She was tired and wasn't sure if she could take too much more. Mirielle assumed the woman was going to to insult her then take her to some hidden castle or fortress where she would be kept until after the curse was to be broken. Along the way, she would be told about all the fiendish plans and how beneath her the mermaid princess was. If Mirielle had her voice she'd just tell her nemesis to 'get it over with.' She didn't care much for melodrama.

The sea witch narrowed her dark eyes at the insolent girl. "I shall teach you some manners!"

Without so much as a finger twitch, a cage of ice formed around Mirielle. The girl grasped at the bars in a panic before a large wave picked her up, carrying her out to sea.

Chapter 33

This was bad. *If I were to rank this on a scale of one to ten, this would be a twenty.* Mirielle cringed as she shivered from the cold radiating off her icy cage. She had to get out, but how? Her mind flitted to Dmitri. He didn't even know where she was. There was no possible way he could help her. It wasn't like she could scream for someone to come to her rescue. Her nose wrinkled at the idea of being a damsel in distress. The idea of it didn't sit well in her stomach, but there wasn't anything she could do at the moment to improve her situation.

She thudded the back of her head against the bars. *Wait… It's made of ice.* Her lips curved into a smile as she unsheathed her rapier then slammed the hilt against the bars. Mirielle grinned as she heard a satisfying crack. She didn't need anyone to save her. She could do it herself!

Metal versus ice. Metal wins. It didn't take too long before Mirielle managed to break enough of the bar to wedge herself through. She was rather pleased at finding no trace of the sea witch.

Mirielle wasted no time in launching off her frozen platform and into the waiting ocean below. She never knew how invigorating it was to outsmart a foe until that moment. She felt elated.

You're not out of danger yet! Bringing her focus

back to her escape, she swam as fast as she could in the opposite direction she had been taken in. If she was lucky, she'd be back on the beach before her muscles started aching.

The water grew violent around her, thrashing against her body as she fought against it. The temperature dropped several significant degrees, but Mirielle continued her battle. She wouldn't give up, refused to.

"You should just surrender. You will never make it."

The blonde swimmer gritted her teeth against the voice. She could feel her muscles cramp up, yielding to the order. Pushing the pain to the back of her mind she kept swimming, making the movements as automatic and mindless as possible. It was the only way she could avoid drowning.

Mirielle bit her lip as she began to lose conviction. The voice was doing its best to make her fold. Despite not wanting to be manipulated, yet again, she found it harder to resist each time. Her own inner arguments seemed ill crafted and pointless. The urge to give in was just too strong.

She felt her limbs go lax as she began to sink, her body at last surrendering to the voice in her head. Now, it was up to the sea to decide what to do with her.

As she began to go under, in the back of her mind she thought she heard someone call her name.

Chapter 34

Mirielle's eyes flew open as she felt herself being yanked to the surface. She gasped in surprise at the sight of familiar green eyes staring down at her.

"Are you okay?" Dmitri held her tight, searching her face for any sign that she was not. Once he received a nod of confirmation he swam her back towards the shore.

Mirielle released a breath, grateful that they had been reunited. She was afraid that she'd never get to see him again. Just the simple thought made her eyes fill. She refused to cry though. She just wanted to make it back on land so she could find some way to apologize.

It didn't take long before they reached their destination. Mirielle let out a mute gasp of surprise as Dmitri lifted her into his arms. She recovered enough to hold on to his shoulders as he moved her away from the water. A twinge of disappointment hit her in the stomach when he settled her against a palm tree. She wanted to hold onto him, but part of her was afraid that he'd reject her, especially after she had left him. Mirielle gave him a tiny smile, hopeful that he didn't hate her. She wasn't sure if she could handle it, not after everything she had just gone through.

Dmitri pulled away then took her hands in his as

he looked her over. His face turned scarlet when he noticed that her skirt was much shorter. Choking from the shock, he peeled his eyes away. "Wh-What happened to your dress?"

Her eyes widened, then she flushed, feeling rather awkward. She wished she could talk so she could explain her trials and tribulations, but was still not granted the ability.

"Were you attacked?" Dmitri checked for any other injuries, briefly glancing down at her legs.

She bit her bottom lip, shaking her head. Perhaps chopping off the skirt wasn't such a brilliant idea after all. It wasn't obscene by normal standards, but this was a different world with more archaic standards it appeared.

"Well, I don't know what happened to your dress, but at least you are all right. We can find you something else to wear later."

Mirielle bobbed her head. She was glad he didn't seem angry, but still felt guilty over having run off like she had. Using her index finger she carved into the sand one simple word, 'sorry.'

Dmitri blinked, in confusion for a moment before narrowing his eyes as though the memory just hit him. "You mean for leaving?"

She nodded, unable to meet his gaze. Pouncer mewed before leaping out of his hiding place. He hopped onto Mirielle's lap, purring with happiness at seeing her. She couldn't help but smile at the kitten as she scratched under his chin.

"It's all right. I didn't know if something was wrong or if you were just sick of being around me." He shrugged, then gathered his coat Pouncer had been nesting in from the ground and draped it over Mirielle's legs. "I wouldn't have blamed you if that was the case so don't worry about me being mad. I'm not."

Mirielle frowned at his words. They were the last thing she expected to hear from him.

"So, you aren't hurt at all?"

She shook her head.

He let out a breath of relief. "I'm glad. I'd hate for anything to have happened to you."

She hesitated a moment then wrote, 'What about you?'

His eyes narrowed at the question and he rubbed at the back of his neck. "I'm fine. Just been looking for you."

Pouncer meowed as though disagreeing.

Dmitri glared at the feline. "Most of the time, when I wasn't... I wasn't sure if you wanted to be found."

Mirielle gave him a smile and wrote, 'Thank you for helping me.'

His face reddened, but he nodded. "No need to mention it. If you're feeling up to walking, we should keep going. We don't want to get caught by whoever murdered Fenton, plus there is your quest to accomplish."

She bobbed her head, giving the prince the sign that she could travel. He helped her back to her feet. She took a few testing steps, satisfied that the needles which had pained her before were gone then looked up at him. Her heart skipped a beat to see that he was gazing down at her. She handed him back his coat, which he stared at before breaking out of his stupor.

"Right!" Dmitri tore his eyes away as he took his coat back. After putting it back on, he then bent down trying to hide the deepening flush as he picked up Pouncer. He hesitated a moment before taking her hand as he led her deeper into the jungle.

Chapter 35

$\mathcal{S}$he felt content. Despite not having any leads on where to go, at least she was no longer alone. Now Mirielle was walking hand in hand with Dmitri. Her fear of him hating her had been extinguished, lifting the heavy weight she had been carrying since she realized how stupid it was to run off the way she had.

"Ow! Pounce! What in the world is wrong with you?" Dmitri rubbed at the back of his neck, scolding the kitten who clawed his way down the back of the prince's shirt.

Mirielle felt herself tense up at the tabby's behavior. Something was wrong. Either they were about to be attacked or something evil was stalking them. Either way, she unsheathed her rapier. She wasn't sure how capable she would be in a battle, but she had to try.

Dmitri noticed the blonde's defensive stance then armed himself with his cutlass. He angled himself in front of Mirielle, his green eyes scanning their surroundings.

Please let it be nothing, she thought, turning her focus to over her shoulder. If Dmitri insisted on covering her from the front, then she would watch his back. It was pointless after all for two people to not guard one another.

Mirielle didn't realize she had been holding her breath until her lungs began to scream for air. She inhaled slowly despite her anxiety over the potential threat. At least she wasn't alone. It was a small blessing in what could be a dangerous situation.

Something snapped near the bushes behind her. Dmitri pulled her back as he whirled around, weapon ready to strike.

This doesn't feel right. Mirielle thought. She turned just in time to block an attack on the unaware prince. She was thankful for her reflexes, otherwise Dmitri would have found himself impaled by a sword.

The greasy assassin smelled like rotten fish as he snarled, "You made me miss, wench!"

Three more men, just as disgusting at the first jumped out at them, surrounding the pair. Dmitri stayed close to Mirielle, ready to lash out at anyone who dared to touch her.

A chubby one licked his lips as he leered at the blonde girl. "She looks tasty."

Her heart hammered in her chest as she stood, watching them with uncertainty. Could they be the ones that had murdered Fenton? Just the speculation made her stomach turn. No, she couldn't think of that. The important thing was to keep them from harming her and Dmitri.

Mirielle kept a firm grip on her rapier. She still was not confident in her fighting skills, but she refused to stand around doing nothing. She couldn't turn her back on Dmitri after everything he had done.

The rank smelling pirates sneered as they approached the pair, each had a weapon of his choice in hand. Then when it seemed as though all they wanted to do was threaten their targets, they sprang.

Dmitri had to throw himself to the ground as a battle axe almost took his head off. He chanced a glance at Mirielle who was fending off a dagger wielding man who liked to aim for the belly. The prince jumped to his feet, slashing another man who was jabbing at him with a spear. The blade of Dmitri's cutlass sliced into the grubby man's shoulder and he cried out in pain.

Mirielle ignored the scream, concentrating on her own fight. The man with the sword seemed eager to run her through, but she was too quick with her evasions for him to so much as knick her with his blade. It was almost like some strange dance she realized, avoiding strikes from her two attackers until she turned enough that sword wielder, impaled his partner instead of the graceful blonde girl.

"Jimmy! Look at what you made me do!" The enraged man watched his friend gargle as blood filled his mouth. He then turned back to the girl lashing out with erratic swings that Mirielle had a harder time avoiding.

Fearful, she struck out as well and gaped in shock as the man ran into the tip of her rapier. It broke through the skin in his throat as he yelled in pain before collapsing, choking to death on his own blood.

Mirielle collapsed to her knees, staring in horror at what she had just done. Even though they were bad, she still wasn't used to taking other peoples' lives. She doubted she ever would be.

Her blue eyes lowered to where the corpses were and widened in shock. Rather than bodies of men they were now fish! She shoved backwards, crashing into Dmitri's legs as he finished off the last assassin.

"Careful!" He said, bending down to steady himself by placing his hands on her shoulders. "What has you so... afraid- What in the world?"

His plopped down next to her in shock as he took in the dead bodies. Absently he took Mirielle's hand,

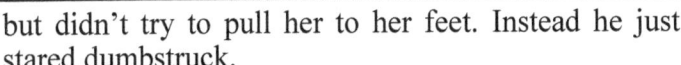

but didn't try to pull her to her feet. Instead he just stared dumbstruck.

After a moment he recovered. "We better get out of here before something even more disturbing happens. Come on…"

Mirielle didn't protest as they rose to their feet together then raced away from their battleground. She hoped that was the last of the odd occurrences.

Chapter 36

*M*irielle and Dmitri had run until they felt as though they couldn't anymore. She wasn't sure if it was the world or the particular place they were trapped in, but she knew none of it had happened in the story. The idea of dead humans turning into fish was still too much to comprehend. Then again, she was supposedly a mermaid, but that didn't mean she'd turn into sushi when she died, did it? The very concept was disquieting on a whole new level.

"I hate to say it," Dmitri began from his place against a tall palm tree. "But I think our best bet is to go to my home. Fenton may be gone, however, that doesn't mean that all his notes are lost."

Mirielle gave him a small smile as she nodded. She could tell by his demeanor that home was the last place the prince wanted to return to. The fact that he was making the suggestion for her made her heart flutter. No one ever considered her needs above their own. The idea that Dmitri was willing to do so made her feel warm inside.

"All right, then we will look for either a boat or someone, preferably not trying to kill us, that could tell us how far away we are from my parents' castle."

Pouncer seemed pleased with the idea as he perched on Dmitri's shoulder purring away. The little cat's tail twitched with satisfaction when Dmitri scratched behind his furry ears.

"I guess the vote is unanimous. Let's head off again. Maybe we'll get lucky for a change." Dmitri rose to his feet then helped Mirielle to hers. She gave him an appreciative smile, which made him flush in response. He kept one hand wrapped around hers as he led them further into the dense jungle.

Mirielle chewed on her bottom lip. She had never held hands with a single person for as lengthy a time as with Dmitri. She didn't mind it and could admit to herself that she enjoyed it. For some reason, she felt safer. To a degree, she might even say she felt a bit of happiness. Add in the fact that he had kissed her... she didn't know what to make of her bubbling emotions other than she liked his company and had no desire to part from him again.

She could say without a doubt that she could not recall ever feeling anything like it before. She hoped it would last.

Dmitri pushed through a mass of low hanging vines then came to a dead halt. He squinted through the foliage then gasped. "That- that... That's the castle! We're still in Oceanvale!"

What? Mirielle's jaw dropped at the sight of the castle in the distance. It didn't appear too far away, which meant as long as they didn't run into any trouble, they should make it there in a short amount of time.

"I guess it's now or never. Come on," with that he began walking in the direction of his childhood home.

Chapter 37

The closer Mirielle and Dmitri got to the castle, the more uneasy she became. Her stomach felt as though there were a million goldfish swimming in circles, making her feel nauseated. She couldn't seem to shake the anxiety that was consuming her.

The prince at her side squeezed the hand he was holding. "You'll be fine... although your skirt might raise a few eyebrows. Don't worry. They'll love you. Me on the other hand... We'll just see."

She gave him a sideways glance. Why was he unsure of how the people at the castle would feel seeing him again? Weren't they family? She knew he resented being the younger of the twin brothers, but she didn't expect there to be more disdain than just that.

Dmitri's lips curved into a frown as he looked at her hair. "Your comb is gone. I guess it slipped out when you were in the water. It's okay. Maybe we can find another one."

Mirielle touched her hair. She was saddened over having lost the pretty gift. She had never received anything like it before. Most accessories were practical like hair bands. The fact that it came from Dmitri... she couldn't help, but be disappointed in herself for having lost it.

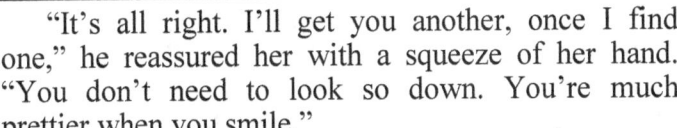

"It's all right. I'll get you another, once I find one," he reassured her with a squeeze of her hand. "You don't need to look so down. You're much prettier when you smile."

That comment made the blonde blush. It was amazing how Dmitri seemed to have the ability to cheer her up with a few simple words. She hoped she could do the same one day.

They walked towards the shore. The castle was a short distance away, but Dmitri began dragging his feet. He rubbed at the back of his neck, the anxiety radiated off him in waves.

Mirielle wished she could say something to provide him with some comfort. Knowing that she could only do so in actions, she threaded the fingers of their clasped hands together and gave his a gentle squeeze.

His eyes shifted to hers. The uncertainty tinged with fear, which had been swimming in his green irises dissipated as his mouth formed a small smile. "Thanks."

She nodded, happy to have been able to help. That joy faded as they passed through the gate. Dmitri's hand fell from hers at the sight of several frozen statues scattered around the courtyard. He stared at them in horror for a moment before breaking into a sprint through the open castle doors, almost dragging Mirielle behind him.

"No!" He cried out in anguish as he came to a dead halt in the throne room where his family stood frozen in place.

Mirielle paused at his side, taking everything in. Shocked expressions were etched onto the faces of the figures frozen in place. Most were men, but she could make out a couple of women. She guessed that one of them was Dmitri's father and the one that bore a striking resemblance to her traveling companion had to be his twin brother. By the brother's side was a pretty young woman. Mirielle couldn't help, but share in the grief. They seemed like a nice family.

Her attention shifted to that of the floor. What should have been tile, was quickly forming a layer of ice. Mirielle pulled on Dmitri's hand in a desperate attempt to yank him away from the impending danger.

It took a moment for him to look at her then he too noticed the floor. He swiped at his face and with her hand still in his, raced for the doors before they could meet the same fate.

Mirielle breathed a sigh of relief once they made it back onto the sand. Dmitri collapsed then beat his hands against the ground. She just watched him with her face a washed in melancholy. She couldn't help feeling the overwhelming sensation of guilt rush through her.

"That's right. If it wasn't for you, his family wouldn't be covered in ice. This is all your fault, you miserable little girl. The only one that deserves the blame, is you."

The blonde clenched her teeth together as she covered her hands over her ears. She didn't know why the venom filled words were being used in her voice, but she couldn't allow herself to fall victim to it. Not again. *You're not going to make me bend to your will, whoever you are. You aren't me!*

Mirielle was so distracted by the laughter echoing through her head that she didn't see the large tidal wave until it was too late. All she could do was brace herself as it slammed into her. She could hear Dmitri cry out her name before she was pulled away into the ocean.

Chapter 38

*H*er lungs screamed for air as she struggled to reach the surface. Mirielle tried to recall how she had wound up in the water, but came up with nothing. Instead, she pushed all her effort into swimming, before she could drown.

Just as she was ready to say goodbye to the world, she freed herself from her watery grave. She drew much needed breath into her lungs then leaned her head back, focusing on inhaling and exhaling. After a moment, she lifted her head, scanning her surroundings. Panic flooded her as she realized that nothing looked familiar. In fact, she couldn't see anything except for water.

No, no, no. This can't be possible. Land has to be around here somewhere. I couldn't have drifted out in the middle of nowhere! Mirielle slapped the water in frustration. This was bad. How was she supposed to find Dmitri, let alone the Crystal Garden if she was stuck in the middle of the ocean? She really screwed up this time!

Calm down. Don't freak out... too late. Mirielle squeezed her eyes shut. She knew she'd be lying to herself if she said she wasn't scared. This wasn't something that she considered normal. Then again, neither was being whisked off to some strange land and being told that she was a mermaid princess from a fairy tale.

She reopened her eyes and glanced around. There had to be something to give her a sign as to where land was. Even a mountain peak would be enough. After a thorough search, however, she was left unrewarded. Mirielle let out a silent groan of frustration. She knew despite being a strong swimmer that she couldn't tread water forever. She also didn't want to drown.

A thought she had fought to deny surfaced to her mind. If she was the Little Mermaid, then that should mean she might be able to breathe water. Then again, she had legs so did that mean she no longer had the ability?

Mirielle shook her head. She had to stop thinking about the fairy tale. It was clear that the story did not match up to her reality. She couldn't rely on it for answers. For once in her life, she'd have to believe in herself.

"You are a fool if you think that," her mind chided.

She shook her head again. No, she couldn't let that negative voice pull her down again. She had already caused too much trouble. She needed to trust what she felt deep inside, despite the fear that wanted to choke her. Mirielle didn't want to turn her back on Dmitri. She had to believe in the faith he had in her. Too much was at stake for her not to.

Mirielle inhaled as much air as she could then allowed herself to sink. She closed her eyes as she concentrated on her heart. *I am the Little Mermaid. This is my world and I will find a way to save it.*

A warmth flooded her as the water swirled around her. In shock Mirielle drew a breath then gasped, realizing that she wasn't sputtering. In fact, she didn't feel the need to resurface. It was as though she were floating in the sky rather than in the water.

Something glowed a brilliant blue a few inches from her. She reached a hand towards it and almost jerked back realizing that it was a rose that looks as though it had been carved from a large sapphire. _Is this..._

Mirielle pressed a finger against it, staring in bewilderment as it disappeared. Her lips curved into a smile as images flashed through her mind. She remembered. She really was the mermaid princess. Her gaze shifted down and she laughed at the sight of her tail. She would survive.

No sooner had she had that thought, did the water begin to freeze around her. Mirielle had to escape before she became a mermaid ice cube!

She swam as fast as she could. To her surprise, it was even faster than when she had legs. With one strong push, she managed to breech through the surface, flipping in the air, before crashing to the hard ice below her.

Mirielle groaned then pushed herself upright. She clenched her teeth, realizing that she was still unable to use her voice. Was it too much to ask to get it back at the same time as her memories?

Pushing those thoughts aside she focused on her magic, using it to give her back the legs she knew she could still use. In a brief whirl of water, she was back to her feet clad in an off the shoulder dress of deep blue which bled to that of an aqua color. It was shorter in the front with a longer skirt in the back. She wore silver shell encrusted sandals on her feet, and around her head was a matching diadem with blue stones along it. She smiled at her reflection, happy to feel more like herself at last. Now, she just had to take care of her nemesis.

She let out a heavy sigh. She was not looking forward to facing the sea witch again. She only hoped that Dmitri and the rest of his kingdom would be all right. Time was running out fast. If she didn't find some way to break the curse soon, everything would be engulfed by Mirielle's beloved ocean and she refused to let it happen.

Mirielle squared her shoulders and was about to hunt down the sea witch when the voice started screaming in her head. Pained, she clutched at her ears, as she dropped to her knees. All she could hear were the shrieks before she lost consciousness.

Chapter 39

This needs to stop happening. Mirielle groaned as she lifted her head. Rather than encountering Lunette as usual whenever she passed out, Mirielle instead found herself in what looked like an underground cavern. The stone walls were shiny with moisture, glittering like polished crystals. It was an odd sight, considering she had no idea how she got there.

Mirielle pushed herself to her feet. *At least that stayed the same.*

Despite being able to transform into a mermaid, it was a welcome sight to look down at her dress knowing that there were a pair of legs under the skirt. It made her feel less like a beached whale. Now she just needed to figure out where she was and how to get out.

Mirielle shoved her damp hair from her face. She frowned at hearing water drip from somewhere above her. That meant the cave was either underwater or had a source of water streaming from above it. She was grateful that she wasn't claustrophobic. That would have been a huge problem. Luckily, she never had a problem with confined spaces.

That still didn't help her situation. She still had no idea where she was or how to get back to Dmitri. She hoped he was all right and was not panicking up a storm on the beach. At least Pouncer could provide some comfort.

Think. There has to be a way out of here. I just have to find it. Mirielle climbed to her feet and took a couple of cautious steps. She was relieved that her feet didn't seem to slip on the wet stone. The fact that they didn't perplexed her. The single reason she could come up with was that the soles were made of some sort of special non-slip material or something. Either way it was nice not having to worry about breaking her neck.

Her blue eyes roamed around the cavern. It was dim, but not dark, which meant light had to be coming in from somewhere. She could tell that the crystals' glow wasn't enough to cast the same amount of brightness. Not knowing what else to do, Mirielle pushed her shoulders back then began walking as far as she was able along the walls.

After a moment she glanced up then stopped. There was a large hole on the ceiling of the cave. Could she have been dropped in? Mirielle scowled at that concept. She should have gotten injured if that was the case. It looked like too long of a fall to walk away unscathed. No, there had to be another way. Otherwise she'd have to sprout wings and fly because the stone was too slick to climb up.

Mirielle sat down on the ground, folding her arms over her knees. What use was finding her rose if it was no use to her? It was frustrating to think that she had just unlocked her memories only to remain trapped. At that moment, she really wished she could scream.

Her ears perked at the sound of dripping water. *Wait… that's the answer. I have the power over water. Maybe I can use it to get out of here!*

She stared up at the hole, pondering if she had to use a source provided or if she could create her own.

She decided to trust her gut. Focusing on her hands, she made a circle of water that soon developed into a water spout. Still concentrating she increased its size until it was high enough to reach the hole with little effort.

An ocean breeze brushed through Mirielle's hair as she inspected her surroundings. Her lips turned downward into a frown at seeing no sign of the castle. *No matter. I'll find my way there. I will make amends.*

Mirielle felt a tear fall from her eye as she leaped off the cliff, transforming back into a mermaid right before she hit the water. She would make everything right again somehow. Her mind shifted back to her recovered memories as she swam. At least the surrounding water was already salty.

Chapter 40

The sacrifice was worth it, Mirielle decided, making her way to the shore. She could remember the last time she had seen her mysterious human and longed to be reunited once again.

His dark hair was shining in the sunlight as he stood on a large floating object in the middle of the ocean. If what she had heard from her sisters was correct, it was called a boat.

It wasn't long before the sky grew dark, and water fell from it in great torrents. The wind whipped with great violence as streaks of light crashed down followed by angry roars.

The blonde didn't know if this was a natural occurrence so she continued gazing at the man until the line on one of the masts snapped, plowing the massive beam into the person of her affections, sending him into the ocean. Mirielle didn't think, she just reacted, diving below the surface after him. He was heavy and almost dragged her down with him, but she refused to give up. Using all her might she dragged him on shore. It wasn't long until he coughed up the water he had inhaled.

Mirielle was torn between staying by his side or fleeing back into the watery depths of her home. She chose the latter in fear of how he would react to her being a mermaid.

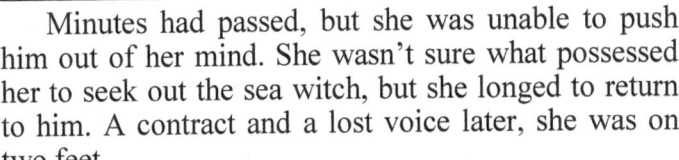

Minutes had passed, but she was unable to push him out of her mind. She wasn't sure what possessed her to seek out the sea witch, but she longed to return to him. A contract and a lost voice later, she was on two feet.

Mirielle had difficulty adjusting to her new legs. It was awkward trying to balance on them. Even more so she had never felt so exposed before. The sea witch had not offered her anything to cover herself with and Mirielle had never thought to ask.

It didn't take her long, however, to find the person she had been looking for, or so she thought. The human had turned a deep shade of scarlet at the sight of her then withdrew his coat covering her with it.

"Do you mind my asking, what happened to your clothing?" He inquired.

She opened her mouth to respond, but no words would come out. Instead she smiled, shaking her head.

The man gave her a pitying look. "I see. I guess it must have been dreadful if it has made you mute. If you would like, you can come with me. I'm sure someone can find you some clothing."

Mirielle nodded then together they walked to the castle. She was ecstatic at seeing so many different things that her companion had to tie his coat around her to spare her modesty.

He waved at a woman who had greeted them. "Can you fetch this poor girl some clothing? I found her wandering on the beach. We might need to take her to see Fenton. She might be in a state of shock."

"Of course dear." The pretty brunette held out a hand to Mirielle. "You can come with me."

The blonde hesitated a moment then accepted the offered hand. It didn't take long before she was clothed in a white peasant top with a dark blue corset with a teal and blue print skirt. As the woman who she was told was named Lillian, brushed Mirielle's long blonde hair she began gushing.

"Isn't Nicholai such a gentleman? To think you were left in such a state. Naked of all things! I cannot imagine what happened to you, but you can rest assure that you are safe here." Lillian grinned then showed off a sparkling ring. "You are so lucky to have come here. This kingdom is the most peaceful and I should know since I'm marrying into it. I am in such disbelief! Nicholai and I will be married in just a matter of days."

Mirielle felt tears well up in her eyes at the startling news. Her mystery man, the one she had fallen in love with, was engaged to another. She had given up everything just for him and now it was all a waste. She managed to compose herself enough to sit through the rest of the woman's chatter.

It wasn't long before she was escorted back through the castle gates with food and money in hand.

"I hope that's enough," Nicholai said giving her a friendly smile. "If you ever need anything, please don't hesitate to ask. Our kingdom after all, wishes to have all of its citizens happy. I wish you the best."

Mirielle smiled, despite the tears wishing to fall as her heart shattered with each breath she took. She watched Nicholai give her a wave. She then turned on her heel trudging back to the water unaware she had just sentenced her people and the seaside kingdoms' to death with her selfish act.

Chapter 41

Mirielle gritted her teeth as she swam faster. She had been such a fool! Bargaining with the sea witch despite the warning had cost her not only her family, but her people as well. She could still remember the sea having turned redder the deeper she swam back to her home. All around her was nothing, except death. Her parents, her sisters, her friends, were gone. Massacred by evil. All because she had released the sea witch like a genie in a lamp!

She had been warned not to treat the octopus figurine she had found in her father's vault like some sort of wish making object, but she set free the entity concealed within anyway.

"You wish to return to the surface…" The strange woman like creature said as a statement rather than a question. Her dark red lips were curved into a knowing smile as her dark hair flowed around her.

"Yes! I want to meet the human I had saved," Mirielle nodded then like a naïve child, she agreed to drink the blue potion the sea witch had conjured up in exchange for her voice.

Mirielle cursed herself for being such a complacent idiot. She had been blinded by love and suffered the ultimate price. Now that she knew it was Nicholai not Dmitri whom she had given up her voice for, she couldn't help feeling confused over her affections for the twins. She knew Nicholai was in love with Lillian, but the fact that he was the reason she was in this mess was disconcerting, considering she now had feelings for his twin. To add insult to injury, it was also her fault that Dmitri had lost his ship.

I shall make it up to him. Somehow.

It was funny to think of the illusionary world she had been in. Instead of possessing a single memory of having a family, she had been discarded all together. Now, knowing that she had a family only to have lost them, twisted the knife even deeper. She would make the sea witch Claudette pay. Their deaths would not be in vain. Not as long as she breathed.

Mirielle clenched her teeth. She could think about vengeance later. Right now, she had to find Dmitri before the evil witch did something to him. *Please still be alive.*

With that being the mermaid's sole focus, she sped up her pace, cutting through the water like a dolphin. Dmitri just had to be okay. She refused to accept any other possibility. The mere thought that he could be dead was enough to make her ill. *No, he's alive. He's got to be.*

Her lips formed a smile at the sight of the castle in the distance. It would not be long before she was back. Once she was reassured that Dmitri was safe, she'd work on bringing the sea witch down and breaking the curse. She only wished she knew how to go about the process. Then a thought occurred to her. The castle residents may be frozen, but if they could get back inside and avoid being frozen over then perhaps they might find the solution to saving everyone.

It was worth the risk and now with her water magic, it might be easier to keep herself and Dmitri safe. With that in mind, she pushed herself even harder. This was one race she would not lose.

Chapter 42

The coarse sand stuck to Mirielle's damp legs as she ran along the beach. If she had a voice she would have called out Dmitri's name. Instead she did her best to scan her surroundings in hopes of catching sight of him. Her breath caught in her throat at seeing no trace of the dark haired prince.

Don't give up hope. He's got to be around here somewhere. Mirielle took strength from her thoughts. She had to stay positive. Anything else would be like tempting fate. She would find him. She had no doubt in her heart about that.

Swiping her long blonde hair away from her face, she continued trudging up the sand bank, back to where she had left the prince.

Her face fell at finding no trace of him. *Maybe he went to the castle?*

Mirielle turned to go back into that direction when several shadows caught her attention. She spun around to find six men, all dirty looking and smelling like rotten fish. A few of them snickered as they circled the mermaid princess.

"Look at what we got here… a lost little girl," the rotund bandit of the group chuckled to himself. He waved his sword at Mirielle as he gestured to her.

His lanky companion nodded, licking his lips. "Good enough to eat."

Mirielle cringed, wishing she could back away, but they had circled around her. Without anyone else to aid her, she'd have to save herself. At least she wasn't defenseless. That was something she was very thankful for.

Let me go and I won't harm you! Mirielle attempted to say, trying to look as threatening as possible, but was unable to utter a single word. Her eyes widened in horror at having been caught in such a state.

The men laughed at Mirielle's predicament. It was obvious that her silence the last thing they expected. She watched as their eyes gleamed with a predators' thrill marking her as helpless prey. Even if there was someone who could aid her within earshot, they would never hear her cries.

"Look's like it's our lucky day, boys," the hulking man to her left snickered, reaching out a beefy hand towards the small defenseless blonde.

Her lips curved into a smile. She anticipated her reaction would throw them off guard. With a sharp movement of her hands, she slashed out at them with a whip of water.

The bandits drew back in shock. The burlier of the bunch recovered enough to try striking her with his axe. Mirielle evaded then concentrated on her magic to summon a weapon. A beautiful rapier encrusted with pearls and seashells formed from a burst of water in her hand.

With quick, graceful movements she struck back, attacking with a combination of her weapon and a whip of water. The men faltered back in disbelief, they turned on their heels; then fled. Before they could reach the water, a cage of ice formed around them.

Mirielle kept a tight grip on her rapier as she watched her attackers fight to free themselves from their prison. It wasn't long before the ice snaked its way up their bodies, freezing them in place. She narrowed her gaze as her nemesis rose from the ocean water. *Claudette.*

The sea witch took one look at the mermaid princess then laughed. "Do you really think you can defeat me child?"

Yes, was Mirielle's silent answer. She would win this battle once and for all. She wouldn't back down until the sea witch was no more.

Chapter 43

*M*irielle pointed the sharp end of her rapier towards the sea witch. She wanted to scream out 'You tricked me!' but knew no words could pass through her lips. Instead she fixed her most violent glare upon her nemesis.

"Oh, come now, dear. If it wasn't for me, you wouldn't have gotten acquainted with that fetching prince!" Claudette smirked at the hesitant look on the girl's face. "Or was it his brother you were after?"

The princess shook her head. She couldn't allow herself to get distracted. That was what the witch wanted. She had to defeat her then find a way to break the curse.

Mirielle barely had enough time to react to the ice shards sent her way. In a quick flick of her wrist, she summoned a funnel cloud of water to lift her out of harm's way. It was strange how easily the water magic came to her when she thought of it, but she couldn't risk pondering on it for long. She had to stay in the moment.

"So you have found your flower... It will do you no good. You will be mine, little princess." The sea witch remarked before launching more ice shards at the blonde haired girl who managed to dodge the assault.

I can't do this forever. I need to get the upper hand

somehow. Mirielle decided, distraught over her ill advantage. She didn't know how effective her attacks would be against the woman. Could Claudette freeze her water attacks? It was alarming to consider that her own magic had the potential to be used against her. *Focus!*

The reality of her situation was that she was afraid. This was the monster that terminated her people. Who was to say that she was just playing with Mirielle until ending the mermaid princess's life in the same savage manner? After all, Mirielle was the one who had set the sea witch free.

"Perhaps a *fair* fight would suit you more. Why don't you meet some of my former clients? They had a lovely visit with that old hermit you met at that little hut." The sea witch cackled as she gestured to a group of men and women who appeared from the sea foam.

Mirielle's stomach clenched. Is that what would happen to her if she didn't break the curse? Was her fate to become a slave to the sea witch?

"Poor little one… You didn't read the fine print on our little contract, did you? Such a shame. You were so insistent to find your sweet prince that you didn't pay attention to what you were signing away. Too late now. It's just a matter of time before you are mine forever."

How could I have been so stupid?

"Oh, and before you start tormenting yourself with endless berating… you had the ability to have legs on land all along. You just needed to strengthen your magic to do so." Claudette sneered at the stunned mermaid before her. "Basically, you handed over your voice and life for nothing!"

Chapter 44

The rapier shook in Mirielle's grasp as she took in the sea witch's words. Was it true? Did she have the power to walk on land all along? The mere thought made her sick to her stomach. If Claudette was truthful then that meant everything was Mirielle's fault. The deaths, the curse... all of it. *Don't think like that. You can make amends... somehow. Plus that may be nothing, but lies for all you know!*

Mirielle squared her shoulders, drawing in a deep breath. She couldn't give up now. She just hoped that Claudette hadn't gotten her claws on Dmitri. Her eyes wanted to tear up at the corpselike figures shambling up the shore. She didn't want to harm them unless it was necessary. Then again, if what Claudette said was correct, they were the ones who were responsible for Fenton's death.

She had to make the right decision. Looking at Claudette's former clients, Mirielle realized that they were barely alive. Reanimated bodies being puppeted by the sea witch herself. The idea of it made a shiver roll down the blonde's spine. She never wanted to suffer their fate and doubted they wished it for themselves. If she destroyed them, it would be merciful.

With her mind made up, Mirielle slashed at them with a whip of water. It made the bodies stagger back, giving her enough time to capture them in a water spout, before putting them out of their misery with a few well aimed stabs with her rapier. As she set the corpses down, they had taken on the form of fish rather than humans.

"I see you have learned a few tricks…" Claudette murmured, having witnessed the mermaid princess execute her minions. "You will be a splendid pet indeed."

Mirielle wiped her blade on the sand, her gaze never parting from the sea witch. She wished she had her voice back. There was so much she wanted to say, but couldn't. She couldn't ask why or even about Dmitri's whereabouts. Instead she was at Claudette's mercy as far as information was concerned. It just infuriated her more.

"Poor sweet little, princess… Are you sad that your voice is gone? You should be more careful with what you wish for," the sea witch mocked, tossing her dark hair. She sneered and with a wave of a hand, she rose from the water on a set of legs of her own. The dark green dress flowed behind her as she strutted onto the beach with an ice spear in her grasp. "Perhaps it will just be more enjoyable to end you. After all, you are almost extinct."

Don't let her shake you. She's just trying to catch you off guard. Mirielle held her rapier out as she slid into a guard stance. Her attention was so focused on the sea witch that she didn't noticed the attack from behind until it was too late. She felt pain flood between her shoulder blades before everything went black as she collapsed to the sand. Her nemesis's laughter echoing in her head.

Chapter 45

Mirielle's eyelashes fluttered, a soundless groan passed from her lips before she opened her eyes. She blinked, then frowned. Where was she? Pushing herself upright, Mirielle discovered that she was sitting next to a river in the middle of a meadow. Birds chirped from the trees as forest animals played. It was rather serene. She couldn't help, but smile as a rabbit hopped by her.

Then a terrifying thought popped into her mind. Was she dead? It would explain the surrounding peace. Her heart ached at the thought of not being able to see Dmitri one last time.

"What are you doing here?"

Mirielle spun around to find an auburn haired girl around her age with hazel eyes staring at her, her brow arched in a skeptical expression.

The mermaid princess winced, being unable to answer. She tried to mime that she couldn't talk, but only received an eye roll.

"That's a likely story."

"It's true," a familiar feminine voice said, joining the pair.

Mirielle was relieved to see that it was Lunette. At least she could explain to the other girl what was going on.

The red head studied her companion and nodded,

her stance relaxing. "You have my apologies. You can never be too careful after all."

Lunette laughed. "She will learn soon enough. As will you."

Mirielle's brow knit together at the girl's words. As she turned to see if Lunette might explain herself further, the world seemed to spin and a moment later, she was no longer outside, but in a white room. *How can this be possible? What is going on?*

The room was unlike anything she had seen before. Circled around it were six pedestals. Four were lit up in either white, green, pink, or blue while the others had crystal roses in red and purple floating above them. She blinked in surprise. Was this the Crystal Garden? If so, then why was she here? Hadn't she already received her flower?

"I was wondering when you would show up," a young woman with wavy brown hair wearing a shimmery blue dress said, stepping towards Mirielle. She held a large gold ball in her hands then smiled. "I am Orina. The Guardian of the Water Rose, your rose to be exact."

The blonde nodded then gestured to her throat, indicating that she couldn't talk.

Orina smiled in understanding. "I know. I have been watching you. I am the guardian of your flower after all. Despite what you may think, you have not fulfilled your duty yet. You still need to break the curse after all, but I can assure you that it won't be easy. You will have to push past all your insecurities and find your inner strength."

Mirielle sighed. This quest was proving to be far more troublesome than she anticipated. Being unable to talk seemed to increase the difficulty even more so than if she hadn't forfeited her voice.

"Now, I have to warn you to be more careful.

Claudette is far craftier than you might have imagined. It took everything in Lunette to pull you out before you could die. Ice blades to the spinal cord is not a good thing. You might experience some pain when you wake up though, but that will be the worst of it." The brunette stroked her ball in thought. "Breaking the curse will be tricky. However, I believe you are capable of it. And no, I do not know how exactly. That is something you must discover. Just work past your insecurities, then you'll be fine."

The blonde nodded, studying her companion with care. There was something about Orina that made Mirielle uncertain and a bit melancholy. She just wished she knew why. Pushing that thought aside, she gave the young woman an appreciative smile.

"Take caution. You will have to make some difficult choices. Do not fail," Orina warned before the room dissolved around Mirielle in a haze of blue.

Chapter 46

A gasp escaped Mirielle's throat as she jerked upright. Her back was killing her, but somehow she was able to move. When she blinked, her lips formed a frown. Why did everything that was not near her look distorted? Did her eyesight go bad?

She tried to stand then wobbled, unable to get her footing. That was when she realized that she wasn't standing on the ground, but in a bubble!

What in the world? Mirielle reached a finger to the curved wall nearest her and touched it. It burst a second later, sending her crashing to the ground a few feet below her.

Dazed, she glanced around and blinked in confusion. Wasn't she previously on a beach? The bright green grass and colorful flowers did nothing to lessen her bewilderment. If anything, it was giving her a mild panic attack. *Where am I? How did I get here? Did I float here? How do I get back?*

She winced as her head began to hurt. This was not good. How was she supposed to defeat the sea witch if she was in a forest of all places? She needed to find her way back to the ocean.

Mirielle sucked in a breath through her teeth as she shoved her hair off her back. It provided a minor amount of relief. She hoped it would stop hurting soon. There was no way she could fight in such a condition.

Breathe. You can do this, just don't think about it... She urged herself to take a step then wished she hadn't. Just the movement alone had tears flooding her eyes as she released a silent scream. It was too excruciating to go any further. Defeated, Mirielle dropped to her knees, wincing with agony.

"Are you all right?"

Mirielle lifted her blue gaze at the sound of an unfamiliar female voice. She blinked in surprise at seeing a girl with raven hair wearing a blue gown staring down at her from a white mare. Sitting astride a chestnut colored horse was a man with his blonde hair pulled back into a ponytail. He opened his mouth to say something, but she stopped him with a simple touch of her hand.

The girl slid off her horse, her curls bouncing with the movement, then approached Mirielle. "I think I recognize you. You have the Water Rose I think. I am Bianca or better known as Snow White, and this is my fiancé, Alphonse."

Of course. Dark hair, pale skin... it fits. Mirielle nodded and gestured to her throat.

"I think I understand. You lost your voice, but you look to be in far worse pain than just that."

The young man joined her side, peering down at the girl sitting on the ground. He circled around and blew out a whistle, his face edged with concern. "Bianca, you might want to take a look at her back."

The dark haired princess met her fiancé's gaze. Her eyes widened for a moment then she did as he suggested. "Oh my! No wonder you're in pain. Your back is blistered with what almost looks like frost bite. Did someone do ice magic on you?"

Mirielle nodded her head, hissing out a breath through her teeth as Bianca touched the damaged skin.

"I have never seen anything like this before... I can try to undo the damage, but I don't know how successful I will be. I might make it worse." She bit her lip in fear of hurting the blonde girl.

Mirielle lifted her head then nodded, hoping she got the message across. Even though she didn't know Bianca, she was like her. If anyone could heal her, it was another chosen of the Crystal Garden.

"Okay. Alphonse, do you have a handkerchief?"

The young man frowned as he unearthed one from his pocket. "Why do you ask?"

"She may need to bite down on something. Also, if you don't mind holding her hand, it may help in dealing with the potential pain."

"Are you sure you want to do this, Bianca? I mean, yeah it's noble of you, but what if something goes wrong and you end up hurt instead or as well?" Alphonse looked at the ground, as though trying to hide his uncertainty.

His fiancée gave him a gentle smile, taking his hand in hers. "If she doesn't break the curse on this land then everything we have done means nothing. I have to try even if it is dangerous."

"I'm not going to pretend that I am happy about this, yet like usual, you have a point." Alphonse sighed, giving in.

Bianca smiled and gave him a chaste kiss in gratitude. "I shall be careful, I promise."

"You better," he said offering Mirielle his handkerchief before taking one of her hands in his.

Bianca drew a deep breath then released it. "You might want to think happy thoughts and brace yourself."

Mirielle nodded as she shoved the handkerchief in her mouth and closed her eyes. It didn't take long for her to draw up Dmitri in her mind as she reflected on their moments together.

"Here we go," the dark haired princess muttered then using her ice magic, pressed her hands to the exposed part of Mirielle's back. She gritted her teeth, maintaining focus.

Pain. Pain. Pain! The mermaid princess clenched the handkerchief in her mouth with her teeth as she kept a death grip on Alphonse's hand. She felt like the skin was being peeled away layer by layer. Tears streamed down her face as she fought to ignore the pain, but it was too much. She wished more than anything she could pass out... until it all stopped. Mirielle opened her eyes, stunned at being unable to feel anything.

"I think... that should do it." Bianca murmured. Her voice sounded a bit weary, but she was smiling. She rose to her feet and stumbled. Alphonse barely had a chance to grab her before she fell.

"Are you all right?"

She bobbed her head. "A little tired. I haven't used my magic in a while. I'll be fine."

Alphonse lifted her into his arms, not even giving her the chance to argue. "I warned you."

"But it worked. Am I right?" She looked at Mirielle for confirmation.

Mirielle felt herself soften at the exchange. It was obvious that Bianca and Alphonse cared a lot about each other.

She rose to her feet and took a few steps. Having felt no pain she spun around for good measure and let out a silent giggle. She wished she could thank Bianca in some form.

"To repay me, when you break the curse, seek out Lunette. I'm sure she's been helping you, but she will need our aid when her time comes. In the meantime, you must break the curse that was set in place here at all costs. Can you do that?"

Mirielle bit her bottom lip, yet nodded. There was far too much at stake to turn her back now.

"Wonderful. Then we shall meet again," Bianca gave the blonde girl a smile as Alphonse lifted her onto her horse.

Yes, we shall. Mirielle gave the couple a wave and started off through the woods. She couldn't waste any more time. She had to find a way to break the curse and hopefully, along the way find Dmitri. Until then, she would just have to do her best on her own.

Chapter 47

*M*irielle was relieved that her bubble had sent her not too far from the castle. If she could sneak inside, perhaps she'd be able to find something to give her a clue on how to break the curse. All she had to do was avoid being turned into an ice sculpture. Easy right?

She pursed her lips in thought. There had to be a way inside...

As she stared at the castle, an idea popped into her head. *What about enclosing myself in a bubble? If it floats then I won't touch the floors except when I need out of it to grab something.*

The more she considered it, the more Mirielle decided that it was worth a shot. She just wasn't so certain about how to create one, let alone make it move. She blew out a breath in agitation. She could do this! She needed to figure out how.

Mirielle closed her eyes, trying to imagine a bubble forming around her. *Please work...*

She felt her feet leave the ground and almost smiled. When she glanced down, she could see the sand a few inches below her. So far so good. Now to figure out how to make the silly thing move on command.

Do I just imagine moving? To test her theory, she thought of the bubble lifting higher. To her delight it did just that. *This will save on travel time!*

With her new mode of transportation, Mirielle directed her bubble to the castle, floating right through the gate. She paused in the Great Hall. She had no clue where to go. She knew Fenton's room would be the most logical place, but Dmitri never told her where it was located. To make matters worse, given the size of the castle, she could be wandering for hours!

So much for my brilliant plan, Mirielle decided in disappointment. Torn between which ways to go, she decided to try left. She frowned at the sight of yet another corridor. This was going to be a long day.

Mirielle glided her bubble further along. So far, so good. The ice didn't seem able to touch her. As she passed another door, she heard a shout not too far from where she was followed by a high pitched meow.

She didn't think and instead directed her bubble towards the source of the uproar. If she had a voice, she would have let out a happy squeal at the sight of the prince and his cat clambering up a bookcase to avoid the approaching ice.

Despite not knowing if her bubble would pop or not, Mirielle reached for Dmitri and as her bubble burst, formed another one around each other.

Dmitri stared at her in utter shock. "You- you're here, but how- We're in a bubble?"

Mirielle gave no warning as she threw her arms around him, grateful to be able to see him once again. She wanted to ask what had happened after she had been taken away, yet knew that would have to wait. For now, she was content being close to him again.

Dmitri froze for a second, as though needing to comprehend what was happening. He recovered, tightening his grip on her, returning the embrace. His fingers tangled in her long hair as he murmured, "I thought I was never going to see you again. Glad to be proven wrong."

She pulled away then caught a joyful Pouncer who all, but cried against her neck. She lifted him up and stroked his soft orange fur.

"You look different- Not that it's a bad thing," Dmitri added, his face coloring in a flush over his careless words, but was unable to remove his gaze from her. "It's just- Wow, that color bring out your eyes."

Mirielle smiled as she blushed in return. She still wasn't used to the compliments, but wouldn't say no to them either.

"If you're wondering what I'm doing here, I'm looking for anything Fenton might have left behind on the curse. He has to have some notes on it somewhere."

That made Mirielle excited. They were thinking the same thing.

Dmitri dug into his coat and unearthed a thick tomb. "I found this before the room decided to attack me. I don't know if it has what we need, but I figure it's worth flipping through."

She nodded in agreement then moved closer so she could peer over his shoulder as he flipped through the book.

From the looks of it, it was a journal of sorts. The handwriting was messy, yet legible. Most of the pages were filled with rambling thoughts, sketches on possible inventions, and a few theories. Just when they were starting to lose hope, they came across what they were looking for.

"This is it! It says the only one that can break the curse is the mermaid princess—you. In order to do so… she must sing." Dmitri's voice dropped as he said the last part.

Mirielle was so disappointed in herself over the

news that the bubble burst around them. Before she hit the ground, Dmitri managed to catch her. Rather than smile at him as she usually did, she pushed him away. Despair was flooding her. She had really messed up this time! She was the only one who could break the curse and like an idiot, she had given up her voice!

In frustration the blonde shoved a stack of books off the table then fell upon it sobbing. She had let everyone down and there was no way to fix things. So much for keeping her promises. She was such a screw up!

Dmitri placed a hand on her shoulder. "We'll figure this out. There has to be some way to get your voice back. You can't give up yet."

She shook her head, refusing to lift it from the cradle of her arms. *You're wrong. I have doomed us all. I wish I could fix this, but I can't. We're all going to die and it's all my fault!*

"Mir, look at me." He shifted his hand to her back, rubbing it in gentle circles. "We will find a way. I'm going to help you with this."

Dmitri stepped away then grabbed a quill, ink bottle, and parchment. He put the quill in her exposed hand. "Mirielle, talk to me. Please."

She scrunched her eyes up, then sniffled a few times. She didn't want to look at him. He'd hate her if he knew the truth. *You did this to yourself.*

Mirielle drew a breath, deciding to get the inevitable over with. He wanted to her to talk. She'd do it, but in the end, he'll regret ever asking. With a deep sigh, she set quill to ink.

Chapter 48

Shame washed over Mirielle as she stared at her words. Dmitri wanted the truth, he got it. Now, he knew who she was, what had happened to her, and that she was the reason they were cursed to begin with. Unable to stare at her handwriting any longer, she shut her eyes, awaiting the prince's rage.

After a long moment of silence, Dmitri finally spoke. "You were tricked. Not all of this was your fault. To be honest, we all do stupid things. Myself included. You just need to push the guilt down and try your best to learn from your mistake."

Mirielle kept her eyes closed. She wanted to ask him if he hated her now, but was too much of a coward to do so. She flinched when he put a hand on her shoulder. She didn't deserve to be comforted no matter what he thought otherwise. Mirielle swallowed hard then stepped away from him.

"Mir... I'm not mad at you if that is what you think. You've been through a lot and like I said, you had been manipulated." He pounded a fist on the table. "It's not like you acted like a complete jerk and left the moment your brother's engagement was announced!"

She looked at him, surprised that he had shared something personal with her.

Dmitri gave her a half smile. "Nicholai wanted me

to be his best man and I gave him the cold shoulder as I walked away. It was bad enough seeing you mooning over him when he brought you to the castle. I bet Lillian put a damper on that."

Mirielle felt her eyes water with the memory. She felt like such a fool for having fallen for some strange man that turned out to have been engaged.

"He may have been the one who had found you after you gave up your voice, but I was the one you saved from drowning." The look on Dmitri's face was bitter as he glared down at the floor. "You see, Nicholai hates the water. It's a wonder he was on the beach when he found you. So you didn't give up your voice for him like you thought. It was for me. The fault is shared, Mir."

Her jaw dropped. If she was able to talk, she wouldn't have been able to find the words. It was all too startling to discover that Dmitri was the one she had fallen in love with all along. She just didn't know if he felt anything for her. She wouldn't allow herself to test the theory. She would just continue working together with him and maybe, after they break the curse, she would let herself consider how he might feel about her. She knew he cared for her. That was enough.

She returned to the parchment and began writing as a single solution came to mind. She knew it would be hard and she might die, but it was the only way.

Dmitri read over her shoulder then blew out a breath. "If killing the sea witch is the only way, then we have no choice. Let's go find her."

Chapter 49

Mirielle and Dmitri left the castle to find a place that wouldn't turn them into ice sculptures. It didn't take too long before they found a secluded forest a ways from the ocean. They sat together on the grass with some food that they had found in the kitchen which had not spoiled.

Dmitri bit into an apple as he glanced at Mirielle's parchment. They had taken as much as they could along with ink and quills, packing it and extra food in a bag. "So you can do water magic?"

His blonde companion nodded her head. She sipped at one of the flasks they had packed. She nibbled on a biscuit in thought then jotted down, 'But the sea witch seems to have ice magic. I think I'm at a disadvantage.'

He scowled at her message. "There has to be some way to defeat her. We just have to come up with it."

Mirielle shrugged and glanced over to Pouncer who was inhaling his fish. She picked up her quill again. 'Maybe it'd be easier to find an antidote for the potion she had me drink.'

Dmitri shook his head. "I don't think we have enough time for that. The waves have been getting rougher. I think it's a sign of the curse. It won't be too long before they're taller than the castle."

She nodded then sighed. Taking another bite of her

biscuit she chewed in thought. Her magic couldn't be completely useless against Claudette. It just didn't seem right, being the Chosen of the Water Rose. So how was she supposed to use it to defeat the sea witch? Would sticking her in a bubble work or would Claudette be able to pop it?

"Anything? I can tell you're thinking. You do this little nose twitch…" he said, demonstrating. "Though you look more adorable doing it."

Mirielle could feel her face color but wrote down her thoughts.

Dmitri's brow arched at the word bubble. "That is a good question. Can someone else pop your bubble?"

She moved to write some more, only to have her hand caught by the prince. She lifted her gaze in question.

"Why not do a test? Try putting me or Pouncer in a bubble and see if we can get out."

Mirielle blinked in surprise at the suggestion. They may lack magic, but anyone could pop a normal soap bubble. What if hers were more durable? It was worth a try. She nodded in agreement then gasped as he helped her to her feet.

"We're ready when you are."

She looked at Dmitri, holding a less than thrilled Pouncer then gave him a small smile before she focused on them to form a spherical shape around them. It took a bit of effort, but she did it. The prince and cat were in a bubble. The prince reached a finger towards the inner rim and poked it, but nothing happened. This made the kitten freak out, turning his tiny claws on the bubble. Still nothing.

Mirielle smiled before setting them free.

"It worked!" Dmitri cheered as Pouncer returned to his abandoned meal. "I know, it doesn't mean its magic proof, but still, we have something we can try."

She let him enjoy the small victory as she sat back in the grass and munched on a strawberry. In the back of her mind, Mirielle feared that Claudette would be able to escape the confinements. Time would tell.

Chapter 50

"So now that we know how to deal with the sea witch, any idea about what song you need to sing when you get your voice back?" Dmitri inquired, making Mirielle look up from her food.

She hadn't considered that. What do you sing to break a curse? She grabbed Fenton's journal and flipped through the pages in rapid succession. *There has to be something in here!*

Dmitri put a hand on her shoulder when she tossed the book in frustration. "Maybe it doesn't matter what you sing or it might be a song you already know."

Mirielle rubbed at her eyes, wishing that for every answer she received, she didn't end up with five new questions. It was aggravating! Her gaze dropped to her lap where Pouncer decided he wanted to cheer her up, pawing at her leg as he stared at her with large green eyes. She calmed then picked up the kitten, cradling him against her chest as he continued purring with content.

"See, even Pounce is trying to tell you not to worry," the prince smiled down at her.

She bobbed her head, but wouldn't meet Dmitri's gaze. She couldn't stand the thought of failing. Not after everything she had done. Her family would be so disappointed in her. Especially her father. She would have received a severe scolding for her foolishness.

"Are you all right?" Dmitri murmured brushing away a tear from Mirielle's cheek that she wasn't even aware she had shed. "What's wrong?"

She just shook her head and let Pouncer go before he started complaining about getting wet. Drawing her knees to her chest she buried her face in them. She didn't deserve consoling or kind words. She was a disgrace.

"Mir," Dmitri began, touching her shoulder, which she shrugged away. "I know things are tough right now, but they'll get better."

Unable to talk, she lifted her head enough to grab her quill then scratched out, 'Stop! I don't deserve sympathy. I'm the reason my family is dead. It should have been me not them. I should have died instead!'

He grimaced at her angry words. "You're wrong. Yes, you had let loose the sea witch, but you didn't tell her to commit murder. You are a victim in this. Nowhere in that contract did it specify that you would forfeit your people. She probably killed them so they couldn't imprison her again."

Mirielle sniffled, as she took in Dmitri's words. It did make sense that Claudette would execute the ones who could seal her back up again, that and take her revenge. The mermaid princess drew a deep breath. She hated feeling so weak.

Dmitri rubbed her back, and after a moment of hesitation, wrapped his arm around her shoulders instead. He kept some distance between them, but remained close enough that she wouldn't feel like he was trying to avoid her. "So don't blame yourself. I'm sure your family didn't curse your name before they died. They probably wanted to know if you were all right more than anything."

She nodded, accepting the prince's words.

He removed his arm then rose to his feet and

offered her his hand. "If you're done eating, we should probably head back to the beach. I would think that'd be the place we'd find her, since we don't have access to a boat."

Mirielle took his hand, and together they packed up the rest of their things. Soon, she found herself walking hand in hand with Dmitri once again. She couldn't help, but fear that this might be the last time.

Chapter 51

It didn't take long before Mirielle and Dmitri were back on the beach where the ocean waves had stolen her away. The prince's grip on her hand tightened as though the place brought back disturbing memories. She couldn't blame him.

Pouncer peeked out at the waves from Dmitri's collar. His tail twitched with uncertainty. Dmitri reached up and scratched the cat behind his ears in an effort to sooth him. The feline eased his body, melting into his human companion's neck.

"I don't see any sign of her. For once, I think I'm disappointed," Dmitri muttered as he kicked at a clump of sand. "Figures she wouldn't show once we had a plan."

Mirielle frowned. This was not going as she had hoped either. The sound of the ocean waves didn't seem to offer any comfort either. If anything, they made her feel even more on edge.

Heaving a sigh, she dropped Dmitri's hand and walked towards the shore. Perhaps she needed to become bait in order to catch Claudette's attention. It was worth a shot at least.

"Mir, where are you going?" Dmitri inquired, jogging after her.

She gritted her teeth together. This was her fight. She didn't want him to risk himself on her behalf. It just wasn't right. Mirielle turned to face the prince and made a shooing motion.

He shook his head. "No, I'm not letting you dangle yourself out here like a worm on a hook."

Mirielle winced. She didn't count on him figuring out her plan so fast. Regardless of what he said, she was going to do this. With that in mind, the blonde spun on her heel, then stomped towards the water.

"Mir!" Dmitri grabbed her wrist and tried to pull her away.

Rather than give in, Mirielle snatched her arm out of his grasp and picked up her pace. She had to do this whether he liked it or not! The blonde let out a silent scream as Dmitri snatched her around the waist, lifting her off her feet. She kicked out, trying to free herself without resorting to using her magic. She didn't want to hurt him despite how angry he was making her.

"Calm down," he growled in her ear, keeping a firm hold on the infuriated blonde. He let out a shout as she bucked against him, causing him to lose his balance. Pouncer leaped down, scampering to safety just before Dmitri and Mirielle crashed to the ground. The prince winced, having landed on his back, with the dazed mermaid still in his grasp against his chest. "Ow. You're a feisty little thing. Are you all right?"

Mirielle sighed, remaining still for a moment, her head resting against his shoulder as she lay on top of him. She was tired of fighting against Dmitri. Perhaps it was a stupid idea to tempt the sea witch into attacking her. She nodded her head to his question on her well-being and wished she could ask him the same. Instead she rolled off. Reaching a hand towards the sand, she began writing her question, when the sound of movement caught her attention. Curious, she glanced up then choked. Shambling on the beach were the withered corpses of her parents, sisters, and her other people. Rather than fins, they all had feet and were stumbling towards Mirielle, their dead eyes paralyzing her with fear and grief.

Chapter 52

She couldn't make her legs move. The sight of the dead approaching her was more than terrifying. It was heartbreaking. Mirielle felt her eyes fill with tears, blurring her vision.

"Mirielle, get up!"

She was aware of Dmitri struggling to pull her to her feet and the frightened cries of Pouncer.

"Mir!" Despite his urgings, the mermaid was still frozen in place. Dmitri hissed out a breath then hauled her up, cradling her in his arms in an effort to save her. To his relief, she didn't resist.

They are here for me... She was unable to shake the thoughts from her head. They had died because of her and now they would make her pay. A part of her wanted to face their wrath, yet another was afraid, not wanting to face them.

Dmitri sat Mirielle against a tree then patted her face. "Mir. Mirielle, snap out of it! Come back to me. Wake up!"

She blinked as his hand made contact with her face in a light slap. Her blue eyes met his green ones as he wiped the streaks of tears from her face.

"I'm guessing you knew them." His voice was gentle as he kept his hands on her face so she couldn't avoid him.

Mirielle gave him a nod then squeezed her eyes

closed to prevent anymore tears from falling. The images of the decaying bodies of her family and people were ingrained in her memories forever.

"I know you might feel you are to blame, but you're wrong. None of this is your fault unless you let them kill you. I doubt they would want to do you any harm if they were still alive." Dmitri brushed a lock of hair from her eyes. "Don't let the sea witch make them do something against their will. You have to fight."

The blonde's eyes shot open. She couldn't do that. Not against her family. *Please no!*

"Mir, listen to me. Would they be happy knowing they died then were controlled by the sea witch and forced to murder you?"

Mirielle closed her eyes, but shook her head.

"Don't let them suffer any more than they have. Bring them to peace. Can you do that?" Dmitri stared at her, awaiting an answer.

She returned her gaze to meet his and nodded.

He gave her a sad smile, then stood up, helping her rise to her feet as well. "I'll be here with you. You do not have to face this alone."

Mirielle drew a deep breath in an attempt to regain her composure. This would be the most difficult thing she had ever done in her life. She summoned her rapier, just in case she needed it and with her head held high, approached the hoard.

Chapter 53

I'm sorry. I never meant for any of this to happen. I promise to avenge you all. Please forgive me, Mirielle thought as she looked at her people with great sadness. It pained her to have to destroy their remains, but it would be what they would have wanted. No one should be turned into a puppet against their will.

Dmitri moved to step ahead of her, but she caught his wrist. He looked at her in question. His answer was a shake of her head followed by her pointing to herself. He nodded in understanding then drew back. "I will provide you with back up if you need it."

She gave him a tiny smile in appreciation. With a deep breath, she turned to the animated corpses then using her magic, surrounded them with a wall of water. She felt her heart break into a million pieces with each face that she recognized. *I need to destroy them.*

The best way she knew of was to wear down the bodies until there was nothing left. With that in mind, she created a water spout, right over the sand so it would suck up the gritty sediment. Redirecting it to her captive corpses, she drew them in then began the process of breaking their bodies down. Tears stung her eyes as she caught glimpses of her sisters and father. Even her mother who was nothing more than skin and bones was recognizable.

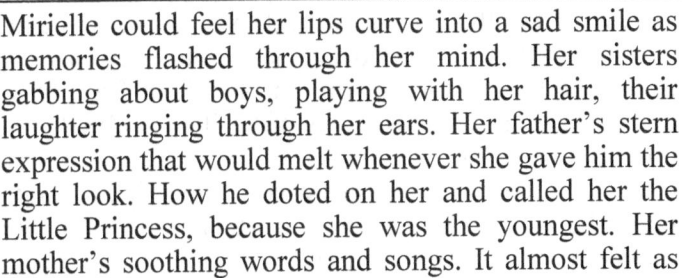

Mirielle could feel her lips curve into a sad smile as memories flashed through her mind. Her sisters gabbing about boys, playing with her hair, their laughter ringing through her ears. Her father's stern expression that would melt whenever she gave him the right look. How he doted on her and called her the Little Princess, because she was the youngest. Her mother's soothing words and songs. It almost felt as though the memories were their way of saying goodbye.

Dmitri put a hand on her shoulder, watching the magic at work. "This is very honorable of you."

She nodded, her eyes never leaving the waterspout. She sighed when at last nothing, but lifeless bones fell to the sand.

"Do you want help in burying them?"

Mirielle nodded, wiping away fresh tears from her face. Together, she and Dmitri moved the remains from the shore, then buried them in the thicker sand where their graves wouldn't be eroded away by the water. She sprinkled a few sea shells over the grave as she knelt in front of it.

Dmitri dusted off his pants, then put a comforting arm around her. "I know it's not the most ideal gravesite and we couldn't bury them separately, but your people were happy together, right?"

She nodded. It was like a large family. Everyone not blood included. And now she was the only one left. It made her shiver to think about it. She wasn't just an orphan. She was the last of her kind.

"You're not alone."

Mirielle winced at the words. It didn't seem fair that she had to lose so much due to one single moment of misjudgment. She felt a sob in her throat, but rather than hold back, she let it out, allowing herself to mourn.

Dmitri said nothing, and sat next to her for a moment, conflicted on what to do before pulling her into his arms, allowing her to cry into his shoulder. He rubbed her back as he whispered, "Just let it out, Mir. Let it all out."

She didn't even realize she was in the prince's arms until she found herself gripping at his shirt. Pouncer moved from his tree then nestled against her neck, wanting to comfort the blonde as well. Mirielle barely noticed and continued crying until she had a coughing fit.

"Do you need water?" He offered her a flask when she pulled away from him, the kitten leaped back to his shoulder.

Mirielle accepted, then gulped it down before Dmitri tugged it back.

"Easy, don't want you getting sick," he said letting her have it again. "Do you at least feel a little better?"

She paused mid-sip considering. The heavy sensation that cramped up her chest had released. In fact, she felt ten times lighter. Shifting her gaze to Dmitri's, she nodded with a small smile. *Yes, I think I'll be okay now.*

Chapter 54

*M*irielle rose to her feet, ready to face whatever the sea witch threw at her next. It was a poor choice of Claudette's to send the mermaid princess's deceased family after her. Facing them again was just what she needed for closure. Now she needed to wait for the sea witch to make a personal appearance.

"Do you believe it's that simple?" the voice berated her, almost making her lose her balance. *"After all, you chose an imaginary world where you are an orphan. Do you think your family would forgive you just like that? What it all comes down to is, you never deserved them. You were meant to be alone and always will be."*

The mermaid princess groaned, clutching her head at the unexpected onslaught of condescending words. *Stop it! You're not me!*

What she received as a reply was a chuckle followed by, *"That is where you are wrong. Why else do I have your voice? You know that I am right about everything."*

Leave me alone! Tears rushed down the mermaid princess's face as she collapsed to her knees, still holding her head.

"Mir?" Dmitri grabbed her the blonde's shoulder in concern. "What's wrong?"

"You are worthless. Nothing except a disappointment. You know that's what you saw in everyone's eyes. Wasted potential. You and your sisters each had their own individual qualities. Yours was failure. You were tolerated and nothing more. They only pretended to appease you. Even Dmitri."

Mirielle shook her head against the loathsome words. *That's not true!*

"Then why hasn't he kissed you since the first time? He's with you in hopes that you will save his people. Once you have broken the curse—if, he will go back to his normal life and you will be left all alone," the voice mocked in a sweet tone. *"No one likes to be around weak, foolish girls who brought about their own families' demises."*

Unable to take any more of the hateful words echoing in her skull, Mirielle slumped to the ground as she lost consciousness.

Chapter 55

Where am I now? Mirielle thought, taking in the familiar white room. She was thankful that her head was no longer killing her and the cold voice had at last been silenced.

"I was hoping I wouldn't see you so soon," Orina muttered as she approached the confused blonde. The brunette let out an exasperated sigh. "If you want to break the curse, you will have to be a lot stronger than that. Passing out is not going to get you too far."

Mirielle winced. Despite not knowing why she was hit with such hateful words or where they came from, she couldn't help feeling guilty.

Orina rolled her blue-green eyes. "And stop putting all the blame on yourself! You were doing well before, but now you seem to be slipping. What is it with you progressing two steps only to take five back? It's aggravating to watch!"

Sorry, Mirielle shifted her gaze to the floor as shame washed over her. She didn't mean to be ruining things. Perhaps the voice was right and she was destined for failure after all.

"Stop that! I know what you are thinking, so stop. You were chosen by the Water Rose for a reason. Just as I was." The guardian whispered the last words before she continued. "So accept your mistakes then move on. Don't let those words of doubt control you.

I know, easier said than done, but you have to at least try to fight them off."

Mirielle bopped her head.

"I know how difficult it is to take all this responsibility. It would be much easier if you could do one thing and that is listen to your heart. You know deep down, that your family loved you. They knew you were destined for great things." A sly smirk curled on Orina's lips as she held up her golden ball, close enough for Mirielle to see it. "Dmitri seems to care quite a bit about you too. If you don't believe me, see for yourself."

Mirielle watched in shock as Orina's ball glittered before showing her what looked like a choppy ocean. She gasped at the sight of a frantic Dmitri, searching throughout the wreckage of his destroyed ship.

"Mirielle!" His voice cracked as he fought through the water, his drenched face was etched with fear. "Mir! Where are you?"

He drew a deep breath and dove below, dodging through the debris. It wasn't too much longer until he had found her. In a quick movement, he swam towards her then hauled her back to the surface. "Are you okay? Mirielle?"

She didn't respond. Her eyes remained closed. Dmitri checked her pulse and cried out in a panic. "No, no, no! You are not going to die on me. Not now. Not after everything!"

Her circled around and released a sigh of relief at finding the beach a few feet away. He swam with all his might until they made it ashore. Lying an unconscious Mirielle onto the sand, he began to apply chest compressions followed by mouth to mouth in an effort to save her life. "Come on, Mir. Come back to me. You can't do this to me. I just found you again! Give me something to live for, for crying out loud!"

When it seemed like all hope was lost, Mirielle at last drew a sharp breath before she began regurgitating water. Dmitri helped her turn onto her side then lifted his face to the sky as he uttered a silent thank you. "Slow, deep breaths. Take it easy, Mir. You're okay."

The scene from Orina's golden ball faded into mist. The young guardian's eyes looked sad as they focused on Mirielle. "Do you not see? The voice is wrong and it's making you afraid of getting close to someone because you think you'll just end up discarded."

Mirielle didn't know what to think. Until that moment she thought Dmitri was only helping her because he either felt obligated or it was just in his nature. She never anticipated that he cared that much for her. It was almost too much to take in.

"You cannot let your own insecurities control you. If you do, you will never amount to anything." There was something about the tall brunette's words that touched Mirielle deep inside. It was as though the girl spoke from experience. Knowing the potential truth made Mirielle's urge to try even harder strengthen. She resolved to break the curse for both of them and if possible, set the guardian free.

Mirielle gave Orina a smile, hoping that would be enough to get what she was thinking across.

The brunette tucked a wavy strand of hair behind her ear, returning the gesture. "I wish you luck. Go find your prince and don't be afraid to express how you feel. I… wish I could have done the same. Maybe one day I will find redemption for my own foolishness."

You will. And I shall help you. The mermaid took her companion's hands in reassurance before she disappeared.

Chapter 56

*M*irielle scrunched up her face, not wanting to open her eyes. She had a mild headache, and her jaw hurt from clenching her teeth so hard. The blonde could tell that she was lying on the ground with something firm under her head. She tried to move, but was given a gentle push back down. Alarm flooded her, until she heard a familiar voice.

"Easy. It's all right. Just relax," Dmitri murmured, brushing back a lock of hair that had fallen in her face. "Take a minute, then you can try sitting up."

She sighed, but did as he asked. Her head was swimming too much at the moment for her push him away. She tried concentrating on Orina's words. How could she, the mermaid princess, be expected to defeat a part of herself? It was all overwhelming.

Mirielle's nose wrinkled as the sensation of wet sandpaper stroked her cheek. She opened her eyes to find Pouncer licking her face as he purred with happiness.

"Pounce, leave her alone. She just woke up," Dmitri lectured the little tabby who meowed in response.

The object of the cat's affections however, ran her hands through the soft orange fur, earning a satisfied string of purrs. Mirielle smiled at Pouncer, glad the kitten was easy to please. A gasp escaped her throat, as she felt herself pulled upright. Strong arms, held her steady until she maintained her balance.

"Are you all right?" Dmitri inquired, unable to meet her gaze as though he were nervous about something. He drew a deep breath then admitted, "These episodes you seem to have, are startling. I wish I knew how I could help you prevent them."

Mirielle gave him a smile hoping that it would reassure him enough. She wasn't sure if it would be proper to hug him or not. She was still getting used to the idea that he cared for her more than she thought. Having never been in a relationship before, she didn't know quite what to do. The idea of Dmitri wanting to be more than friends made her blush.

She watched him stand up, then accepted his offer to help her to her feet as well. He turned away, a slight red shade coloring his cheeks. He rubbed at his face, and looked towards the sea. His hand engulfed hers as he pointed towards the water.

"I don't think we have to worry about finding the sea witch. It looks like she's found us instead."

Mirielle gasped at the sight of the double-tailed woman, towering high above the water on a pedestal of ice. *I'm not ready for this!*

Dmitri squeezed her hand, then looked at her. "I have faith in you. Make her pay."

She drew a breath, and nodded. She had no choice now. It was do or die. At least she knew Dmitri believed in her, if only she felt the same way about herself.

Chapter 57

 $\mathscr{A}$ strong ocean breeze whipped through Mirielle's long blonde hair as she approached the sea witch. She summoned her rapier, her grip firm on the hilt, using the weapon for strength against her enemy. It was up to her to put an end to her nemesis's rampage once and for all. Mirielle hoped her skills would be enough.

"Oh, look. If it isn't the Little Mermaid... Do you expect to scare me with your puny stick?" Claudette cackled, twirling her ice spear in one hand. "What's the matter? At a loss for words? I can freeze anything you throw at me, little girl."

The mermaid princess continued walking, her gaze never leaving the sea witch. If Mirielle wanted her plan to be a success, she had to get close enough to catch Claudette by surprise. If it didn't work... Mirielle didn't know what she'd do. She just knew, she would do anything in her power to make sure that Dmitri survived.

"So you want to fight after all. Very well then," the sea witch smirked and threw an assault of ice shards at the mermaid princess.

Mirielle didn't think, just reacted as she dodged, before throwing a wall of water up in front of her. The ice upon impact sizzled and evaporated.

Claudette's grin fell away. "What did you do?

That should have worked!"

Unless I use hot water, the blonde thought to herself, pleased with her last minute decision. She wasn't sure if she could alter the temperature of her water magic, but had to try. It was the best defense she could come up with.

"Don't think you will win that easily. I haven't even begun yet!" Claudette turned her attention to Dmitri who was standing in the distance where Mirielle had suggested. A feline smile curved over the sea witch's lips as she formed more ice shards, launching them straight at the prince.

No! Mirielle watched at the ice flew towards Dmitri, as he tried to evade them. A split second later, she encircled a wall of hot water around him. The steam was making his hair stick to his face, but it melted the shards before they could reach him.

She let out a breath, relieved to have succeeded in saving his life. Fury boiled in her blood as she redirected her attention to Claudette. *This ends now.*

Mirielle created a wave of water to push herself up to the sea witch's level. Before Claudette could even react, Mirielle formed a bubble around her nemesis, sealing her in.

"Do you think this can stop me? A silly bubble? Don't make me laugh," she snorted, and with a smirk of victory on her face, powered up an ice attack to break her prison. To the sea witch's horror, the ice bounced off the sides then hit her instead, freezing the entire bubble.

Before it could roll, and crash to the ground, Mirielle motioned for it to move above the sand. It did as she requested.

She grinned, happy to have succeeded in defeating her greatest enemy. Just as she was about to spin in triumph, Dmitri caught her attention.

"Now that she's in a bubble, do you think you can lay off the water shield? I think I'm going to sweat to death if I have to stay in here for too much longer." The prince explained, cradling an unhappy kitten in his arms.

Mirielle flushed with embarrassment and dropped the wall.

Dmitri sighed in relief as he shoved his wet hair from his face. His clothing clung to his body, but he looked no worse for wear. "Congratulations."

Mirielle tried to say 'thank you,' but the words wouldn't come out. She scowled, in disappointment. It didn't work. She still couldn't talk. How was she supposed to break the curse by singing? It was impossible.

"It's all right. Now that she's out of our hair, we can figure this out." the princes said, taking her hands in his. "I'm with you on this, okay?"

She nodded, her fear of letting everyone down began to grow stronger.

"We shall find a way. I promise."

"No, you won't. I told you, you would fail. You have doomed everyone."

Everything went black as Mirielle soon lost consciousness again.

Chapter 58

She was floating, or maybe swimming was more exact. Mirielle opened her eyes to find that she was underwater except it didn't look like any ocean she had ever been in before. She rose to the surface and was surprised to realize that she was in fact in a swimming pool.

Curious as to what was going on, she climbed out then frowned at finding herself alone. *Where was everyone?*

Mirielle grabbed a towel and dried herself off. She looked around for her gym bag, but saw no trace of it. *Weird.*

Confused, she walked to the locker rooms where her team was just finishing packing up. Phoebe, the team captain, looked at Mirielle. "There you are. Since you missed practice we decided to give your spot to the alternate. Turns out April is a much better swimmer than you, so you're not needed. Sorry."

Before Mirielle could come up with anything to say, all the girls left. She stared at the empty bench in disbelief. This couldn't be right. She was needed! Phoebe had even said so herself.

"You were wrong."

Mirielle ran out the door, tears stinging her eyes. Why was she so upset? She was considering quitting the team after all. They just made the choice for her.

She was going to leave them!

She came to a halt in front of the pool. *Wait. This isn't right. I'm not a high school student on the swim team. I'm-*

Before she could finish her thought, someone gave her a strong shove into the pool. Mirielle tried to scream as the water filled her lungs making her sputter, then it stopped. She opened her eyes, not realizing that she had shut them, and gaped in shock at her new surroundings. She was home.

The tall coral buildings towered above her as the seaweed waved lazily next to them. Merfolk of all kinds moved around, going about their day as normal. She felt nostalgic just watching them. She swam up to the castle, excited to see her sisters and father. That joy fell away as she heard cruel whispers from her father.

"Mirielle is such a pretentious child. She never thinks about her actions! I knew I should have had a firmer hand with her, but there she goes again, taking something that doesn't belong to her. She would have been better off with her Aunt Doria. Especially after her mother had passed away. I'm too old to chase after her nonsense!"

The blonde mermaid princess swam from the castle as fast as she could. Was that what her father really thought of her? Did he not want her anymore? The mere idea of it broke her heart.

'I told you so. He never loved you. He only put up with you because you were his child.'

Mirielle shook her head, she had no desire to hear or see any more. It was too painful. Instead she found herself in front of Dmitri's castle. She froze in fear, not wanting to be rejected by him as well. Tears filled her eyes as she stared at it in fright.

Please no more! Why are you showing me all of

this? Mirielle thought in distress to the voice that seemed to enjoy tormenting her.

"Because you need to learn the truth."

The mermaid princess shook her head. *No, you're wrong. How could you know anything about me?*

"Simple," a figure said from behind her. "Because I am you."

Chapter 59

Mirielle stared in horror at her own face. It couldn't be true, but the girl had her same eyes, same hair, same nose… everything was an exact copy of Mirielle. They were practically twins. *How can this be? You can't be me. I'm me!*

"I am you too. Only I can still talk," the doppelganger smirked. "I am the part of you that you choose to ignore, yet deep down feel is right. I am your personal fears manifested."

You're just one part of my personality. You can't control me!

"Wrong again. Why else would you be here?" The other Mirielle licked her lips as she looked at the castle. "I'll bet dear Dmitri is going to decide that you're not worth the effort. A pretty face, yes. But you can't talk. He only feels he owes you something because you saved him from drowning. Last I looked, I'd say you are even. Which means, he is free to walk away."

He wouldn't do that. Mirielle thought, trying not to let her knees give. He cared for her. She could tell. There was more to it than just platonic companionship.

Her copy laughed. "Are you so sure? Besides, you are a mermaid, he's human. What are you going to do, swim alongside his boat and make eyes at him whenever he's at sea? And how do you know that he's not engaged as well, like his brother?"

Mirielle shook her head. Her eyes were burning, and she wanted to crumple to the sand. Instead she stood her ground. *No, it's me he wants. Orina showed me.*

"She lies. She manipulated her ball to show you what she wanted you to see so you'd break the curse for her."

You're the one who is lying! Drawing upon her magic, Mirielle slashed at her doppelganger with a whip of water. The attack went right through her opponent.

"Nice try, poor execution."

Mirielle closed her eyes, trying to concentrate on what Orina had told her. She was fighting herself. That much the mermaid princess could tell. There had to be a way to defeat her, push back the insecurities that were thrown in her face. Then it came to her. She looked up at her other self and gave her a reassuring smile. *I accept that you are the scared part of me who was afraid that no one cares. That felt alone growing up with five sisters. We don't have to feel unimportant. We're the Chosen of the Water Rose. That has got to be something. We also defeated the sea witch. And even though it's a bit disconcerting, I think we know that Dmitri isn't thinking about us on a friendship scale. I think it is love. We don't have to fear being rejected or just pretending that those who care never existed. We owe them that much especially father and our sisters. So, please let's stop fighting.*

The doppelganger just stared in complete bewilderment. Mirielle bit her lip then rushed toward her copy, enveloping her in a hug.

We're not alone. We never were.

Mirielle felt a slight hug back before her other self disappeared. She drew a deep breath, at last feeling at peace as the world faded into thick mist.

Chapter 60

A sigh passed through Mirielle's lips as she opened her eyes. She felt herself blush in embarrassment over seeing a concerned Dmitri leaning over her.

"Are you all right? I'm beginning to think I need to find you a doctor... or a priest with how many fainting spells you have," he said shaking his head at her.

She nodded, giving him a huge grin which took him a back.

"Good, because we have bigger problems..." He helped her up then pointed to the ocean.

Mirielle scrambled to her feet as she gaped in complete shock at the sight of several shipwrecks, emerging from their watery graves. The water also looked higher than before. The waves were now crashing into the grass where Dmitri had moved her. She jumped backwards, pained by the acidic feel of the sea foam. She glared at the blisters forming on the exposed skin of her feet. *So that's how I'm supposed to meet my demise... Wonderful.*

"I think it's just a matter of time before we're either crushed by debris or drowned by the sea," he said in a regretful tone. "If only we were able to get you your voice back."

Mirielle gritted her teeth. She knew it was just a

matter of time before they would face the end unless she did something about it. She turned back to Dmitri, wishing she could talk to him. The sea foam burned at her feet, but she ignored it. If she had to die, then she wanted to do one last thing before she left the earth.

With her mind made up, she secured her arms around his neck and kissed him with everything she felt for him. Tears rolled down her cheeks, but it wasn't long before he returned the gesture with just as much passion as she had expressed.

A gasp escaped Mirielle's throat as she pushed him back. A strange tingling sensation burst through her throat. She touched her neck and looked back to her prince with wide blue eyes. After a moment she experimentally croaked out, "Can you hear me?"

The look of shock then joy on his face was all she needed for an answer. "You can talk again!"

She smiled, knowing that this really was the end. She gave Dmitri one last kiss, as she murmured, "I love you too."

Before he could react, Mirielle turned away from him, creating a pedestal of water to face the raging sea coming towards them. She clenched her hands into fists, as she shut her eyes then drew a breath, fighting to come up with the song she needed. *Don't be afraid. You can do this...*

When she opened her eyes, she knew what she had to sing. It was a song she knew deep in her heart, one that with filled of promise, hope, love, and peace. She put everything she had into it and despite the light-headedness that flooded her, she kept going.

The waves that had been towering above her, shank down like a savage beast being soothed by a lullaby. When at last all was calm again, Mirielle's magic gave way, sending her tumbling to the sandy beach below.

Chapter 61

She didn't want to open her eyes. She didn't want to see the destruction she had caused. Tears leaked through her closed eyelids. A whimper escaped her throat as she felt someone smooth back her hair from her face. A gentle kiss to her forehead broke her resolve and she opened her eyes to find Dmitri leaning over her. His expression was gentle as he brushed his knuckles against her cheek.

Mirielle swallowed, wincing at how parched she felt. She tried to push herself upright and paused, realizing that her head was in his lap. Her cheeks reddened. After drawing a breath Mirielle asked, "Did I fail?"

The prince chuckled as he shook his head. "Quite the opposite. Are you all right?"

"Thirsty, but other than that, I seem to be fine." She winced as he pulled her up to where she could lean with her back to his chest.

Pouncer hopped off the prince's shoulder and settled himself in her lap, purring in contentment. Mirielle smiled as she petted his soft fur.

"I'm relieved to hear that." Dmitri pushed the wet strands of hair from her face then pressed his lips to the top of her head. "I was afraid that breaking the curse was going to kill you."

"I thought so too," she admitted. She kept her gaze

focused on the cat. "I'm sorry."

"Don't be. I'm just glad you survived," Dmitri murmured, giving her a tight squeeze then pressed his lips to the top of her head. "I don't want to lose you ever again."

Tears slid down Mirielle's cheeks as she twisted around to return the embrace. "I'm not going anywhere without you. I'm sorry I put you through so much, but thank you for sticking with me. I doubt just anyone would do that... And now I'm babbling."

"It's all right. I like hearing your voice." He lifted her chin and gave her sweet kiss. "You know, you truly are one of a kind."

"Well, I am the last mermaid... At least I think I am." She wrinkled her nose in thought. "I'm not sure if there are any other colonies in the sea."

"Maybe someday we'll find out."

Mirielle smiled at the idea then hugged him tight. She was glad it was over now.

"Dmitri! Is that you?" A young man called out as he rushed towards the prince. He came to a halt staring at the girl in his twin's arms. "Wait, I know her!"

Dmitri sighed as he let go of Mirielle then rose to his feet, pausing to help her up as well. "Nicholai, this is Mirielle. Mirielle, Nicholai."

"Aren't you the mute girl I found naked on the beach?" the older brother inquired earning a glare from his twin.

She blushed bright red upon the memory. "Yes."

"Glad to see you are okay, and clothed for a change," he grinned. "I had no idea that you two knew each other. Wait... was he-"

"No!" Dmitri shouted, interrupting his brother before he could suggest anything demeaning.

Mirielle then spoke up in an attempt to keep Nicholai from jumping to any wrong conclusions. "I was cursed and it left me... voiceless and naked. Thank you again for your help, Nicholai. It was generous of you."

"That's my brother for you. Always thinking of the little people," Dmitri chuckled, teasing Mirielle.

Nicholai looked between the two then scratched the back of his head. "So I'm guessing that the curse has been broken?"

"Yes, thanks to her."

"Oh thank goodness! Lillian has been going out of her mind between that and the wedding preparations. At least I can assure her that it won't get canceled due to all of us dying." He paused then gestured to the castle. "In fact, why don't we go inside and you can tell everyone about all your adventures. I'm sure mother would be intrigued to find out how you met since Dmitri here stated flat out that he would never fall in love."

The younger twin's face flushed. "Nicholai! Shut it before I bury you in the sand!"

"Then you would have to become king and we all know how much you loath that idea..."

Dmitri grumbled under his breath then took Mirielle's hand. "Might as well get this over with..."

"I have another quest to go on!" Mirielle blurted out to the younger prince's relief. "It's to help one of the other Chosen of the Crystal Rose to break the curse on her land. I was told that it would take all of us to help her and I'd like Dmitri to come with me."

He smiled in satisfaction. "I guess we can pay the family a visit then head off. Can't keep the others waiting after all."

Nicholai chuckled, "I wouldn't expect less from you, brother."

Chapter 62

There were so many people! Mirielle lost track of how many relatives and servants were at the castle. Trying to keep track of the names was even more of a challenge. At least she knew a few faces and Dmitri stayed by her side most of the time.

She was surprised to see Lillian, with her curling brown hair pulled back in a bun, gliding towards her. "Hello."

"It's so good to see you again. Nicholai told me what happened. It must have been horrible being cursed and unable to talk!"

Mirielle gave a shy shrug. "I got used to it."

"I don't think I could bear it! I like talking too much." Lillian smiled, pulling Mirielle aside then grinned as she whispered. "Just think, if you marry Dmitri we'll be sisters! I always wanted a sister."

Mirielle laughed at the bubbly brunette. "I don't know if that will happen or not…"

"Don't be silly. He looks at you the same way Nicholai looks at me. He is over the moon for you. It will happen. Trust me."

The blonde blushed, but didn't argue any further. She didn't know what was in store for her and Dmitri, but as long as they were together, she didn't care.

Much of the evening was spent conversing with his parents and brother with stories shared about the twins' childhood, much of which embarrassed Dmitri. Especially the time he got his head stuck in his father's ship's helm.

When at last everyone decided to call it a night, Dmitri escorted Mirielle to a guest room.

"Good news. We will set sail tomorrow," he announced from her doorway, earning a happy grin.

"Wonderful. I want to keep my promise, even if it's a difficult journey," she replied then threw her arms around him. "Plus the chance to be on the water again, even on a boat sounds like heaven."

He kissed the top of her head. "I look forward to it too. You better get some sleep. We have a long day ahead of us."

Mirielle pulled away enough to plant a happy kiss on his lips. "Just something to remember me by. Until then, sweet dreams."

"Only if you're in them," Dmitri whispered before departing.

Chapter 63

$\mathcal{M}$irielle grinned as she put a hand over her eyes at the sight of Dmitri's new vessel, *The Sea Angel* as he dubbed it. She felt a blush over her cheeks at the sight of the mermaid decorating it which shared her face. She knew he wouldn't have it any other way.

"You ready?" Dmitri walked towards her with his hands out to help her board. There was a glow to him that made Mirielle unable to stop smiling.

"Yes, but what if we have to go further inland?"

He shrugged, leading her around his ship. "Then we dock and hope someone will lend us some horses. Otherwise we just go on foot. Will you be okay with that? You are a *mermaid* after all."

Mirielle giggled at the smirk on his face. "I think I can manage. After all, you'll be with me."

"Good, because if you think you're going to leave me out of your adventure then you have another thing coming," he joked, green eyes twinkling with merriment.

"We will have to thank your parents for the ship. It's very generous of them."

Dmitri's face reddened.

"What?" Mirielle raised her eyebrows at him, and he ducked his head, as he rubbed at his chin.

"About that… It's not immediate, and they didn't

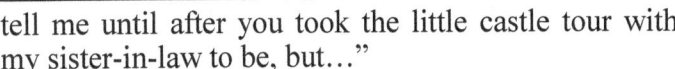

tell me until after you took the little castle tour with my sister-in-law to be, but…"

"Dmitri, spit it out."

"It's a wedding gift!" His face turned an even brighter shade of crimson. "I didn't agree to anything, however, they seem to like you for some strange reason and thought it would suit us best. You don't have to if you don't want to. I don't even expect you to…"

Mirielle threw her arms around him, pressing her lips to his. "Not now, I mean I just turned sixteen. In the future… I might consider it."

He kissed her back. "I would have planned on asking you in a more romantic sort of way, but all right. Then consider yourself engaged. I just need to find a ring."

She laughed. "There's no rush. When you find the perfect one, we'll know when it's time."

Dmitri nodded, accepting her answer. "Well, then. Shall we be off?"

Mirielle caught Pouncer mid-leap then smiled up at Dmitri feeling the most joy she had ever in her life. She was grateful to have someone that made her feel as though she was capable of doing anything. He would stick by her as long as she needed him. They were stronger together and that was what mattered most. Everything else was just details. Their kingdom was the sea, and together someday they would rule it, but first she had to make sure there would be a tomorrow. She would find a way to make sure they would see many more sunrises and sunsets together.

About the Author

LJ Gastineau lives in Saint Augustine, Florida, and is a graduate of the University of Central Florida. She is one of three authors for the website, TrinityGateways.net, and is a co-founder for Trinity Gateways LLC. *Frozen Reflection* is her first published Young Adult novel. She has since published *Quaking Tower*, *Gusty Proposal* and *Drowned Voice* in this series. In addition LJ also has a short horror story entitled *Doll's House* that was published in two adult anthologies: *Dark Things II* from Pill Hill Press and *Shadows of the Mind* from Trinity Gateways LLC.

She is currently working on the fifth book of her Crystal Garden Saga series, *Burnt Wishes,* as well as her cross-genre serial entitled *Hidden Mystique,* which is available exclusively on the website JukePop Serials.

More from

The

Crystal Garden

Saga

The saga begins with

Frozen Reflection

Book 1 of the Crystal Garden Saga

By LJ Gastineau

This would be a birthday she would never forget.

Most girls look forward to their sweet sixteenth birthday. For Bianca Flynn, she believed hers would be an average celebration, one where she would be stuck at home with the stepmother she dislikes. Then things start happening. A strange reaction to apples and an odd phobia of mirrors quickly spirals out of control, throwing her into a world that she thought only existed in stories. So what if she resembles a certain dark haired, pale skinned princess? Fairy tales weren't real. Right?

A mystical quest was not the gift she expected.

After all it isn't everyday that you are swept into a land cursed by a spell that can only be broken with the power of a crystal rose. And there is only one who can fulfill that task, the Princess Snow White.

Turning sixteen has never been more adventurous.

Quaking Tower
Book 2 of the Crystal Garden Saga

By LJ Gastineau

You don't have to dwell in a tower to be isolated.

Cybele Lockley should know. To say that she lived a sheltered life would be an understatement. For as long as she could remember, she had been stuck in a rural house in the middle of nowhere, separated from the world due to a medical condition. Her only company was her grandmother, and just in the morning and the evenings. During the day, she was forbidden to leave the house or even look out the tiny windows. Longing to be free of the isolation, Cybele created a make-believe world in an old notebook, filled with the romance and adventure of a character based on the fairy tale of Rapunzel.

She thought it was just a story…

Everything changes when she attempts to cut her hair for the first time. The room spins, her tawny colored locks grew to nearly three times their original length, the house is transformed into a woodland cottage, and the landscape morphs to resemble an imaginary setting from her notebook. Now she must work to find her true reality – and in doing so must assume the role of her make-believe heroine and complete a quest to find a crystal rose.

This Rapunzel isn't just letting down her hair.

Gusty Proposals

Book 3 of the Crystal Garden Saga

By LJ Gastineau

All she desired was to not be seen as a commodity.

For as long as Violet Piccolo could remember her decisions had always been made for her. From the type of clothes she wore to the friends she kept, she obeyed her parents' wishes without protest, though it chaffed as she grew older. Then, on her birthday, comes the final straw: her father forces her into a relationship with his boss's son in an attempt to advance his own career. Sick of the manipulation, Violet makes a stand for the first time in her life – with unexpected results. To her horror, she isn't just punished by her parents; she also shrinks to a mere few inches high!

Trouble will always find you no matter your size…

The trouble doesn't stop there. The petite girl soon finds herself dragged into another world, one filled with wonder, danger, and magic. Yet while she has been freed from the shackles of her childhood home, she finds herself confronted with others who believe they know what is best for her. To fly free, to discover who she truly is, to achieve her destiny, she will have to learn that sometimes merely standing isn't enough. Some things, she'll have to fight for. And with the aid of a legendary crystal rose, this Thumbelina may achieve all that and more…

It's time to set your sights and aim for the sky.

Burnt Wishes

Book 5 of the Crystal Garden Saga

By LJ Gastineau

Life used to be wonderful...

..when it was just Gabriella Ashton and her widowed father on the family farm. She had wanted for little else in her world, content to tend to the animals and look after her dad. She may have missed her mother, but had no desire for anyone else to replace her.

...before Las Vegas.

One free trip had turned everything upside down. An irritable woman was now the apple of Daddy's eye, and her two daughters were more snotty than nice. In an effort to keep peace in the house, Gabriella retreats into her chores, only to discover her efforts taken for granted by everyone. Frustrated and heart-sore, she tries to make things work — until she reaches her breaking point.

Her world came crashing down to the chiming of the clock.

Bereft and bearing the blame for a tragedy she hadn't caused, Gabriella finds herself alone, wishing things were different. Then a fall throws her from one confused nightmare into another.

Ashes to ashes…

She wakes in a cursed world. Trapped inside the fairy tale castle where a prince swears she danced with him, she's horrified to discover that beyond the walls is a dying land. A preternatural gloom is creeping in, leaving everyone stricken with an insidious plague. While the royal court parties within their isolated fortress, their people are dying.

...dust to dust...

With no way to go back, Gabriella must forge ahead. To do that she must escape. Venturing into the darkness, she will face sickness, death, and betrayal . She must find a cure and burn away the night before there is nothing left but a kingdom of graves.

Time is running out for this Ella Cinders.

Coming Soon in 2015